sweet deceptions

Terri Pray

an erotic romance

SWEET DECEPTIONS

First Magic Carpet Books, Inc. edition February 2005

Published in 2005

Manufactured in the United States of America
Published by Magic Carpet Books, Inc.

Magic Carpet Books, Inc.
PO Box 473
New Milford, CT 06776

Library of Congress Cataloging in Publication Date

Sweet Deceptions By Terri Pray

ISBN# 0-9755331-6-9

Book Design: P. Ruggieri

SWEET DECEPTIONS

Terri Pray

To Karen and Rob for being cheerleaders.

And for my Sam whom I love more with each passing day. I can never say how deep that love goes, but without him, writing would be impossible.

Chapter One

The mists rolled across the open moors, beckoning to her as she stood on the Tor. It didn't seem to matter that she and her people would not live to see the end of the day, all she cared about was the fact she would never again taste his lips as he stole a kiss from hers. She had come to know love and passion both in his arms, but fate had cast them on opposite sides of the powers that struggled for control of her homeland.

The paper crumpled up in her hands and bounced off the wall into the wastepaper basket before she walked to the window. The city stretched out beyond the closed window as Anita leaned against the wooden frame. Somehow she had expected it to be constantly raining, or perhaps foggy, but in her two brief month's stay in London she'd only witnessed a few summer storms. There hadn't even been the slightest hint of fog, or the mist she had tried writing into the ill-fated manuscript, during her stay in the city to spoil the view she now enjoyed.

There was a history within the cityscape that she allowed herself to contemplate… a sense of time, place; an importance that went beyond the brick and concrete buildings she had first expected to see. Dark wood beams and whitewashed walls sat next to Gothic churches with spires that curled their way towards an ever changing sky yet shared the same city block with a plain six-storied office building as if that had been how the city was originally planned. Nothing worked out as originally planned, perhaps that was something she accepted better than others. How many times had she sat down at her computer or with a notepad to work on one story only to have it turn into something completely different by the end of the project? The same could be said for anything in life, from cities to relationships.

There were more stories within the city of London than she would ever have the time to be able to commit to paper, but that had been the very reason she had decided on taking her much needed vacation here. It hadn't worked, though; no matter how hard she had tried to let the stories flow they had ended up the same way. Her muse either refused to answer at all or would show herself in brief flashes that left her frustrated and cursing at the laptop. It was like banging her fist against a door that refused to open. Another relationship that left her frustrated and confused. The very word had become a sore spot with her. The very man she now waited for only added his own abrasions to that tender spot, but she couldn't shake off the hope that Andrew was something more than he appeared to be. More than just a stopgap in her life.

'You're being morbid again,' she muttered to the window as she brushed a strand of hair back from her face and watched her breath fog the glass for a moment. 'Morbid and reading things into the situation that could not possibly be there.' That came with the job description. Possessing an active imagination was both a blessing and a curse when it came to her personal life. All she needed was a quiet dinner, a few glasses of wine, a little conversation, and then she'd be able to put the voices of doubt to rest. There was nothing wrong between her and Andrew that hadn't gained life from her own fertile imagination. He was a good man, she knew that, and just the thought of his light touch sent a shiver through her. His accent alone, that soft cultured tone, was enough to chase away most of her doubts within a few moments of him beginning to speak. So why, when he wasn't here, and especially in the last minutes before he was due to arrive, did the doubts gain such a strong voice?

Andrew Fuller had never shown her any signs of being something other than the strong-willed, kind and sensual man she needed him to be. He wasn't the 'roses every day' type, but he at least called when he was going to be late, dropped flowers off at odd whims, opened doors for her, ordered for her at a restaurant, and he had never left her feeling as though she was anything but a woman he cared for. So why did the voices of doubt manage to gain such strength?

A soft click of the lock from the apartment door opening made her turn, smiling as she pushed the doubts away. Only one other person had a key to the one bedroom apartment she had rented for her stay in the city. Not that they called them 'apartments' here as she'd discovered when trying to rent one. 'Flats' or 'studios' were the terms the real estate agents used.

'All ready and waiting for me, or do I have some rival hiding in the wings?' Andrew smiled, crinkling the corners of his slate-grey eyes. His hair looked almost too neat, combed into place with more care than she paid to her own appearance. That same attention to detail shone through in every item he wore, from the pressed tan slacks to the dark-blue blazer and matching tie. He wouldn't even have needed a mirror to check his hair; a simple glance at the shoes he wore would have been enough. Even though she knew the light-blue summer dress looked good on her, Anita still managed to feel underdressed compared to him.

'Oh, a dozen or more rivals, but they heard your key and took the nearest escape route,' she teased. 'I think one of them is still hanging from the ledge outside. Do you want to check or should we just go for that dinner you've been promising me about for the last three days?' She stopped the playful banter when she saw the momentary frown wrinkle his forehead. 'I'm teasing you Andrew.'

'I know that,' he replied too quickly for her comfort. 'I've been around you long enough to know when you're joking with me or not.'

She doubted that. He'd had problems with her sense of humor from the start, and that frown, however brief, suggested to her that those problems still existed. 'If you say so...'

'Damn right I say so.' He smirked and slid his arm around her shoulders, his fingers brushing the back of her neck before he settled her into his embrace and turned them both back towards the door. She had to wonder if the way he reacted to her comments was the source of the doubts when he wasn't around. 'As for dinner tonight, how about that new Italian place *Gianni's?* I've heard some good things about it so I booked a table for us last week. Soft lights, a private table, some time to talk and discuss plans.'

'Plans?' she asked, but he didn't answer. Italian food, one of her weaknesses and he knew it. England wasn't the void of culinary delights she had been warned about. In just this visit she had dined on Italian, Indian, Mexican, French, German and Turkish foods. So there had also been the English Pub foods, but that hadn't been so bad either, just different. And the chocolate... well that first box from *Thorntons* had been enough to addict her.

'So, would Italian work for you or do I need to cancel the table and find somewhere else?' he inquired a touch smugly.

'You don't hear any objections coming from me, do you?'

'No, but there was no harm in checking. Sometimes it's hard to determine what your mood is or what you might like to do.' He ushered her through the door, letting his fingertips brush along her shoulder, lingering on the nape of her neck long enough to send a shiver through her.

'And what would those "plans" be?' she inquired again, trying to be a little more clear this time.

'I thought that would be obvious as you fly back to the States soon, from what you've been saying.'

'Yes, at the end of next week, which you've always known. You've made no mention about me potentially staying any longer. Has something changed?'

'Well I'm not sure if you've decided to go back to the States or if you want to stay here with me.'

The truth was he had mentioned this before, just small hints, but still hadn't outright asked her to stay. Perhaps she was old-fashioned in some ways, but giving up her home wasn't something she was willing to do without good reason.

'I haven't seen any signs of you packing your bags, but you've not mentioned anything about altering your flight date home, either.'

'There's always a very simple way of finding out what I would like,' she murmured as she locked the door behind her. 'All you have to do is ask.'

'True enough, and then there are some things a man doesn't like to have to ask about, Anita. Some things we like to try and find out for ourselves, others we like to be told about, and even a few things we occasionally like to take.'

She met his gaze calmly. 'And what things would those be?'

'Just a few small things now and then.' He smiled, closing the gap between them. 'A few, shall we say, liberties taken now and then?'

'And just what liberties are you talking about?' she queried, offering him a smile as she watched him.

His smile turned into a darker, almost feral grin as he pushed her back against the closed door and reached for her hands. She could have pulled free, made a scene, even yelled for someone to come help her, but in all honesty she enjoyed the game as much as he did – that show of dominance, with the only risk being someone else walking into the hallway – and when his lips pressed against hers even that concern vanished into the darker recesses of her mind. Her body pushed against his as he growled against her lips, pushing past them, probing the damp confines of her mouth with his tongue. His bodyweight held her pressed against the door, both her hands held by the wrist in one of his as he pushed them high above her head. Even through his slacks and her dress she could feel the swelling outline of his cock, the throb that offered so much more than a kiss and quick grope against the door. Her body knew the delights he could offer, and she was all too aware of the clenching deep within her pussy that left the lips of her sex tingling and moist from the demanding kiss he claimed from her lips.

'We could do a rain check on dinner,' she whispered as he broke the kiss. 'Just unlock the door, stumble back in and-'

'No, I don't think so. I want to take you out and show you off before we come back for the night.'

'You just like to tease,' she retorted. This was the side of him that silenced her doubts and left her feeling both invigorated and excited.

'That too.' He made no attempt to hide his smile as he let

go of her hands and pressed a gentler kiss against her lips. 'Though we do need to talk, and we have that table booked, and it would be a pity to see it go to waste.'

'And you know I don't like waste.'

* * *

'So, do you plan on staying here with me, Anita?' Andrew inquired as he poured the wine for them both. 'Or will you be vanishing back to the States?'

The soft conversation from the surrounding tables melded with the low-key music piped into the room. Candles flickered on many of the tables, and the only other source of light came from the three small chandeliers spaced along the ceiling. Waitresses in starched black skirts and crisp white shirts moved through the widely spaced tables, taking care not to intrude on the conversations of the diners yet still managing to remain within reach if they were needed.

'That's the sixty million dollar question.' She lifted the glass as she returned her gaze to Andrew's face and took a small sip before continuing. 'I have a home there, a life, and I do miss the lake as well as actually being able to work without cursing myself out or throwing things at the nearest wall.'

He wasn't a classically handsome man, perhaps his eyes were a little wider spaced than was acceptable for a model, and there was a scowl that was often quick to take possession of his features, but that didn't matter to her. She had come to know every inch of his body in the last month, how his touch would raise shivering goose bumps across her naked skin before he would cover her flesh with his and slide his eager cock deep inside her clenching sex.

'Ah yes, the famous lake that muse of yours appears to need.' He smiled and raised his glass before tasting the wine. 'Well, we have lakes in this country as well. An entire area of England is named after them – the Lake District. We could take a drive up there this weekend. Maybe seeing that part of the country would help change your mind?'

'And just what would I change my mind about what?' She rolled the stem of the glass between her fingers. She knew what he meant but was enjoying playing the verbal dance with him.

'About you possibly leaving England and leaving me.' He replied as he looked over the rim of the glass at her. 'I'd like you to stay here with me Anita.'

'You could come with me, Andrew.' She suggested as she set the glass down and folded her hands onto the table. She had to go home. 'What's to stop you from following me back home and settling down with me by my lake?'

'My life is here, my work, it's not like yours. You can pack up and do your writing from anywhere. It doesn't work that way with me,' he replied without even appearing to give the idea any thought. 'I can't pack up an office, fifteen employees and everything that goes with it. I have people relying on me, Anita.'

'And I just have editors, deadlines and signings. You make it sound like I have no one at all relying on the work I do, either that or it's simply not that important to you.' She tried to keep the anger from her voice. He hadn't come outright and said her work was *real* work, he didn't have to for her to hear in his voice that he didn't feel it was, but it was real work to her, and to most writers she knew, regardless of if they wrote fiction or on-fiction. 'I need to be home to work at my best,' she insisted quietly. 'I've loved being here, but I do my best work where I'm most at peace with myself.'

He reached across the table, taking her left hand in his own. 'I didn't mean to make it sound as though your work isn't important, Anita. I've seen how much it means to you, just as I know you've tried working over here, I've seen that, but it's not your best work, is it?'

'No.' She wanted to rage at him, push him into a fight, anything was better than him politely accepting her explanation. It wasn't just that, however; he hadn't asked her to marry him, just to stay with him and only with her days there running out had he suggested they visit the Lake District. But her arguments, and the need to fight with him, to give into that temper she had struggled with all through her life, faded with a soft squeeze of his hand. 'No, it's not my best work. It's not even my second best.'

'Maybe it's just being in a city that's the problem?' He leaned back in the chair, his hand slipping away from hers as the waitress approached with their orders. 'We can try the trip north, if you're open to the idea. I've not been up to that area of the country since I was a teenager, but from everything I remember about it I think you'll like it. If anywhere will allow you the time to breathe and write, it's there. If that doesn't work, then perhaps you should think about taking a break from the writing. You could just be burned out.'

She shot him a look. 'I am *not* burned out.' Steam curled upwards from the matching plates, tempting her with the scent of herbs, lemon and carefully prepared pasta as she tried to sort through her thoughts. She had wanted to explore more of the country and hadn't gained the chance beyond a few short trips outside the freeway that circled the city, only they didn't call them freeways here but motorways.

'It was just a thought. So what about it? Shall I arrange the trip or leave the idea for another time?'

There wasn't going to be another time, she knew that. If they didn't take the trip soon she'd be packing and on her way to Heathrow Airport before another chance might arise. Perhaps visiting the Lake District would give them both the chance to relax they seemed to need, and it had been some time since she had looked across a lake whilst nestled in the arms of a man she loved. Who could tell, perhaps she'd introduce him to more than just nestling? She looked across the table, watching the light play across his face before answering, 'When do you want to go?'

'Tomorrow would work for me, though we'd have to make it an early night with the length of time we'd be driving. I should be able to book us into one of the local hotels.' He traced his fingers around the rim of the glass. 'I've no plans for the weekend, and driving that far only to come back on the same day is not my idea of fun.'

'I don't have a problem with staying overnight or with the early night.' She smiled, the tip of her tongue lingering across her lips. Her gaze lowered, following the line of his tie towards the edge of the table before she continued. 'In fact, the early night sounds ideal to me.'

'Maybe you should focus on eating dinner before trying

to help yourself to dessert?' He winked before taking a bite of his meal.

'I always thought it was a pity that I had to wait for the main course before heading for the best part,' she replied, smiling as she felt the heat radiate from her cheeks.

'Then perhaps you should be a good girl and eat up and then I might just see what sort of treat I can arrange for you.' His gaze held hers across the table. 'Though if you don't eat it all up then you could well find yourself across my lap.'

She knew he was teasing, but even so the images his words allowed her mind to create excited her… images of his strong hands, her bare ass upturned across his hard knees, and short, sharp spanks that might lead to deeper touches between her thighs, the warmth of the blows intensifying the heat building in her sex… Her legs clenched tightly together as she squirmed in her chair. She wasn't a submissive, at least she didn't believe herself to be one, but that hadn't stopped her from exploring the occasional light play with the right man. And Andrew was definitely the right man. 'Oh, I think I can manage to eat my whole meal,' she replied before closing her lips around a spear of asparagus to suckle the sauce from it as she watched his eyes grow momentarily wider.

'So it would seem,' he murmured, and shifted in his chair.

* * *

Andrew's hand gently smacked her ass, hurrying her down the corridor, his body pressing closely behind her as she opened the flat door, nearly falling into the room. His hand tangled into her hair, tugging on it as the door locked behind them. His breath warmed her neck, his teeth scraping across her pulse as she clutched his arms, arching into the light bite. Soft waves of shivers left a path across her skin as he pushed her back towards the bedroom. He wanted this as much as she did, the touch of his skin against hers as he pressed her against the sheets. She barely heard the zipper coming down as she leaned into his body, welcoming his kisses, tingling bites and the scrape of nails as they marked a light path across her skin. They didn't make it to the bedroom, but she was beyond caring by the time her dress pooled about her ankles, leaving her standing in her stocking feet on the thick carpet, her garter belt framing her black lace panties.

With a strong grip, Andrew turned her to face him, standing in the long shadows cast by the street lights outside the windows, his face hidden in their depths except for the intensity of his eyes. With a low growl he captured one of her satin covered breasts, squeezing it firmly, his palm caressing her hardened nipple as her cunt clenched with a growing need that threatened to leave her panties moist before he even touched her between her thighs. Shivering, she pressed into his kiss, molding to his body in delight as she felt the throb of his cock through the immaculately pressed slacks, but before she could grasp his hard-on, before her fingers could close around his rigid length, he caught her wrist and turned her around so she was bending over the back of the love seat.

'Now if that isn't a pretty sight…' A sharp slap rang out.

Her hips jerked and pressed closer to the smooth fabric as his low voice whispered against her back, 'A tight satin covered ass ripe for my touch. And what about the delights that lay beneath that satin?'

Her bottom lip caught between her teeth at the feel of his fingers slipping into the sides of her panties. He took his time, easing the lace garment down her thighs as his lips nipped a path down her back, then she stepped out of them as she felt him kneel behind her.

'I never did get the chance to choose a dessert, did I?' His breath warmed her ass, his hands parting her thighs as he spoke. 'All those decadent sweet treats and you rushed me out of the restaurant before I could even sample one.'

Her fingers dug into the love seat, her breath catching in her throat as he slowly licked the length of her damp vulva. Her thighs parted wider, seeking the caress of his tongue. 'Think you've decided on your treat now,' she gasped, her hips rocking back against his face.

'Maybe, though I believe I will savor my chosen sweet...'

His laugh vibrated through her sex lips and against her clit, his tongue curling around her sensitive knob with a quick flick. He was smiling, she could feel that when he captured her clit. She couldn't stop her hips from pressing back against his face, or the way her thighs opened wider as she stood on tiptoe.

'A little nibble here, a small lick there, just to see how long I can make it last. How long do you think it will take before my dessert melts completely?'

'I think you've already managed that,' she groaned, her

fingers grasping one of the cushions for support.

'No, nowhere near that yet, though with a little extra work I believe we could be there soon enough. That's if you have no objection to my eating with my fingers?'

She didn't have the chance to answer before two fingers pressed into the entrance of her slick sex, sliding deep inside her body. With a low groan she rocked her hips back until she could feel his digits fully trapped in her pussy, his fingertips tapping against her clenching depths in time to the deep sucking pressure pulling her clit between his lips. She whimpered, the cushion pulled tight to her breasts as her fingers dug into fabric, each rock back against his hungry mouth pressing her nipples harder against the satin of her bra as he finger-fucked her. She didn't want to wait... each push of his fingers, each wicked flick of his tongue compounded her need to feel his cock opening her up.

'Fuck me!' she pleaded, lifting her head up from the cushion. 'Andrew, please, just fuck me.'

'Oh, I don't think you're quite ready for that yet.' He pulled his fingers from her cunt, tracing them along one tender ass cheek. 'That plea didn't sound quite sincere.'

'Sincere?' she cried. 'How sincere do you want it?'

'How badly do *you* want it?' He licked back from her clit over her labial lips, and then pulled back, leaving her without any of the contact her body blindly craved. 'Do you want it badly enough that you would be willing to get down on your hands and knees for me?'

'I can't...' Her voice shook. He knew that was the one act

he wanted that she had a major problem with. 'Please, you know I can't do that…'

'Then maybe I need to leave for the night.'

He wouldn't do that, couldn't do that, not after the way he had touched her and left her craving his cock buried deep inside her. She turned, trying to plead with her eyes as she reached out a hand towards him, only to watch him step back further out of her reach.

'I want you on your hands and knees, Anita. I want you to do that for me.'

Cruel. There was no other way to describe just how his words felt. He was using her body against her, using the desire burning in her very core to get what he wanted. Any doubt she had that he wouldn't leave her shaking and wanting if she didn't do what he said vanished as she caught a glimpse of the implacable look in his eyes.

Without a word, she stepped towards him. His eyes were intense, his gaze fixed on her face, but he didn't say anything else even as he pointed to the floor. Her legs shook at the thought of falling onto her hands and knees before him, but it was something he wanted, and she wanted him enough to push past her own fears. One thing she had learned about herself was just how slutty being forced or cajoled onto all fours made her feel. There was a shame factor in the act that she had discussed with him when she refused him before, a reaction she feared and desired and shied away from all at the same time. Now she couldn't stop a whimper escaping her, not even when she moved down to her knees and turned around until her ass faced him. Soft waves of deep-red hair tumbled down around her face, covering most of her view. Her thighs parted wide, the stockings and garters and her bra the only clothing she wore as she waited on her hands and knees before him.

Shoes clattered across the floor behind her, pants sliding down to join her dress as he stepped closer. She arched her back, pushing her ass up towards him. She felt him kneel close behind her, teasing the tip of his cock over her sex lips. 'How do you want it, Anita, slow or fast?'

'Just fuck me, please!' She rocked back against his cock. 'Hard, fast, slow, long, I don't care, just fuck me now!'

'Oh, but you do care or you wouldn't be pleading like this.' He held her hips, preventing her from pushing further back onto his cock as he eased his swollen head between the heated lips of her cunt. 'You're a wanton little slut right now, aren't you?'

Her pussy clenched at the harsh words. 'Yes,' she admitted, 'yes!'

'So tell me how you want it, Anita.' He leaned forward, purring the words against her back. 'Beg for it...'

'Fuck me hard, please, Andrew, please, just fuck me hard.' Tears of shame burned in her eyes, but that was all he needed. With a growl he pushed his erection into her begging sex. It didn't matter that his fingers dug in hard enough to leave bruises or that she cried out with the force with which he thrust his cock into her cunt; nothing mattered beyond the claiming of her body with his. She groaned, pushing back against him, her thighs forced wide open as she matched his fierce rhythm. One of his hands pressed between her shoulder blades, pushing her head towards the ground until she felt the carpet beneath her cheek. The firm pressure made it clear she wasn't to push back up against him.

His balls slapped against her labia with each thrust, his grunts merging with the slick sounds of his penis sliding in and out of her juicing pussy. It didn't matter that he held her down to the floor, all she cared about was his cock, her cunt, and their violent desire.

'Tight!' he hissed against her back. 'So tight!'

She cried out, the walls of her pussy clenching around his driving erection as she pushed back against him. She wanted to come, needed to come with him buried deep in her sex, and she needed it now… her fingernails snagged into the carpet, strands of hair caught across her gaping mouth as she gasped for breath, pushing back against him desperately. His cock swelled in her tight hole, his teeth catching the back of her shoulder as she groaned, shuddering beneath him. She couldn't stop it from happening, nor did she want to…

'Come for me!' he commanded.

Her thighs locked as she cried out, the passion torn from her lips as he thrust harder and harder into her body. Even without his command she couldn't have stopped it from happening, nor did she care, not even when she cried out a second time, sinking to the floor trembling as he wrapped his arms tightly around her.

'I'm never going to let you go, Anita. No matter what it takes for you to stay with me, I'll never let you go, not after tonight.'

Her mind wanted to form a protest, but she was too tired to think clearly anymore; all she knew was the feel of his arms about her and the carpet pressing its pattern into her skin as she drifted into a welcome sleep...

Chapter Two

It was barely past dawn when they had headed out from Anita's apartment, Andrew with a travel mug full of tea and she with one full of strong coffee. After spending over an hour curled on the floor together, he had finally lifted her into his arms and carried her into the soft and welcome warmth of her bed without saying a word. Even nestled within his arms she had been treated to a broken sleep filled with ill dreams and questions about both their actions. He knew how she felt about doing it doggie-style, he had to have known just how hard it was for her, yet there hadn't been a single word of encouragement or thanks apart from his declaration that he would never let her go. There had been no words of love or even a general concern as to how she was now feeling. He had been awake some of the night; she had caught him staring at her several times only to see him quickly close his eyes and ignore her whispered words. Yet even when they awoke the next morning there was no attempt to speak about the events of the night before; any attempt to even broach the subject by her had been met by a blank look or outright evasion of the topic. As the busy back streets led into wider roads, and finally onto the London Circular (or London Parking Lot as so many residents of the great city called the M25) she dropped the attempts for a short while, at least long enough to be clear of the city.

It had to be the result of living in a country where trips to anywhere tended to take more than a few hours, but for her the journey from the confines of the city was relaxing. Driving in England had been something she had attempted only when she had to. Between the traffic being on the wrong side of the highway, the change in the sizes of the cars, and the cost of gas, she'd opted for using public transport. With Andrew driving, she at least had the chance to relax and enjoy the change in scenery as they headed north. Well, she would have enjoyed it if he hadn't been acting as if she had some form of plague. If this was a result of them traveling, she was very grateful they hadn't tried it before today.

One thing quickly came to light as the journey continued and she let her gaze play over his face, lingering on the lips that had driven her to the point of madness the night before – he wasn't the type to talk whilst driving, not unless she wanted to count the occasional muttered curse at other drivers. The first few attempts at pulling him into a conversation, other than her probing about the previous night, had only resulted in a grunt or had been ignored entirely, which left her to watch the fields meld one into the other until her eyes drifted close. That had its own drawbacks as she was left to replay the night's events in her mind. For all his passion, his desire, even his demand that she stay with him, he hadn't spoken a word since, as if the night had never happened.

She needed him to speak about it, to talk things through and help push the doubts, the uncertainty and the fear, away, but all she met was silence when she roused herself enough to speak. Three times further she tried to pry his feelings from him only to be met with low grunts, until she gave up and let the steady motion of the car rock her into an unsettled sleep with dreams of Andrew's lips nibbling along her spine as he discussed office politics with a thin blond woman wearing a grey pencil skirt…

Just how long she slept Anita couldn't tell, but when he pulled the car into the narrower lanes weaving their way through the countryside, the change in sound was enough to jolt her awake. Narrow hedges framed the lane as the car sped through the turns, slowing down barely enough to make them safely. 'Where are we?' she inquired once her eyes had refocused and her mind had pushed past the dream.

'About ten minutes outside of Kendal. Thought we'd stop for something to eat before hitting Lake Windermere.' His voice remained colder than she was used to.

'Oh, Kendal? Where have I heard that name before?' There had been something he had introduced her to, a candy of sorts... a hard block of mint candy with a chocolate covering. It had almost been too sweet for her taste. 'Kendal Mint Cake?'

'That's it, used to be a favorite amongst campers and those hiking in the area. It's still pretty popular, though not my thing.' He never took his eyes off the road. Considering the way he was driving she couldn't help but feel more than a little relieved about that. Narrow lanes, sharp turns... it was a wonder he hadn't lost control of the car. The road twisted, growing even narrower as they left the main drag and found themselves on roads barely wider than tracks as far as she was concerned.

'Slow down, Andrew.' She grasped the edges of her chair as he swung around a corner, tires squealing on the tarmac, the car skidding and bringing them close to a low stone wall before he regained control. 'You'll get us both killed if you keep this up much longer. What's going on with you?'

'No I won't, it's about time you learned to trust me, Anita.' He snapped, and turned the car off the road into a small rest area. 'You don't trust me, do you? Be honest about this. You don't trust me at all. I'm just part of the scenery, a welcome distraction during your vacation, a convenient fuck until you head back to your precious lake in America. Tell me something, did you plan on picking up the first man that came along or did you wait a few weeks first? Maybe I'm just research for some more of your precious writing.' His voice was both cold and heartless.

Her throat dried as the vicious words spewed from his lips and there was no way she could avoid seeing the cold contempt in his eyes. He knew she hadn't been looking for a boyfriend, a steady date, or anything more than the occasional companion for dinner during her stay in England, but all those plans had changed when she met him. They had talked about this, hadn't they? They had talked in depth about her plans to go home, about how she didn't want to settle down with anyone right now, and how tumbling almost instantly into bed with him had been completely unlike her. He had even laughed at her shyness and joked about how someone who wrote the type of stories she did could still be so shy, even reserved, except in his hands. Beneath his touch she had let a part of her out she had hidden for years, the part of her who enjoyed being with a man who knew what he wanted in bed, and how he wanted it.

'What on earth brought this on, Andrew?' she asked faintly.

'What do you think brought this on? You went down on to your hands and knees for me. how long have I been trying to get you to do that? I thought that meant you were ready to make a commitment. Isn't that what you said, that unless you were planning on staying with a person you'd never demean yourself by doing that? And now you're still planning on going back to the States, aren't you? After all the time I've spent on you, meals out, time together, even putting other plans on hold for you, right down to bringing you out here, and you've not made the slightest effort to arrange to stay.' His knuckles turned white as he gripped the steering wheel. 'I don't know why I even bothered to bring you here, nothing will ever be good enough for you. I will never be good enough for you.'

Had she implied that if she did that one thing with him it would mean her agreeing to stay with him? She tried to sort through her memories of the conversations they had shared. There had been some odd discussions, but nothing that she thought could have given him that impression. Doing that for him had been difficult enough; even as aroused as she had been the act had still embarrassing for her and the memory of it left her cheeks hot. Now to have the decision used against her, used as an excuse to lash out at her verbally, only contributed to her growing regret. She swallowed hard, looking at him, at the anger in his eyes. In the time they had been together she had only witnessed glimpses of this suppressed rage, hints of the danger it offered, now she saw it clearly for the first time. 'I told you I can't work here, I've tried,' she said at last.

'So the answer is simple enough, give up your work,' he demanded without hesitation.

'What?' Had she heard him right? She couldn't have, he knew just how important her writing was. 'You didn't just tell me to give up work, did you?' She nearly stuttered the words as she felt her hands curl into fists on her thighs.

'You heard me, give up your work. It's not as though it's a real career anyway. Just a hobby, anyone can write that smut.' He looked at her coldly. 'You only write it because you want a real man in your life anyway. Well now you have one so you can drop the pretenses.'

'Are you out of your mind?' She couldn't believe what he had said. Sure, she'd heard the same before from other men, most of the writers she knew had heard it at some point. What woman would write romance for a living if they weren't secretly looking for the right man? 'You want me to give up my writing for you? Not just give up my home, but my work, too, just because you don't think I need to continue it?'

'Yes.' He met her gaze without flinching, seeming not to care just how angry he had made her. 'Yes I want you to give it up. We can figure out another hobby for you, one that you can enjoy over here. Besides, I'm sure once you settle you'll be able to go back to your scribbles without any problems.'

'No, not even if it means never getting laid again,' she snapped. It was taking every ounce of self control she possessed not to reach over and slug him. 'I don't want anything to do with you anymore, Andrew.' Her fingers curled about the car door, tugging it open before he had the chance to put the central locking in place.

'What the hell do you think you're doing? Get back in the car!' he demanded as she stepped out of the vehicle, dragging her purse with her. 'You're making a bloody fool of yourself.'

'Like hell I am.' She stepped back, slamming the door shut in his face as he leaned across to try and catch her arm. 'I'll walk back to London if I have to, but you better not ever show your face in my apartment again. You step foot in it and I'll call the cops. I might not know English law too well, but I'm pretty sure they take a dim view of breaking and entering.' Whatever she had thought had happened the previous night, he obviously had other ideas. She wouldn't have let him bring her out to the Lake District unless she had been willing, really willing, to look at options with him. Had swallowing her pride really meant so little to him?

'You're being an idiot, Anita. This temper spat is not going to do you any good. Get back in the car now and we can talk this through.' He pushed the car door open. 'I'm waiting, but don't test my patience any further, get in the car now before someone sees you.'

'*I'm* being foolish. You demand I give up my writing and I'm the one being foolish? You think I'll just meekly get back into the car with you, sit down like a good little girl and discuss ending my dreams for you?' He seemed more concerned about someone witnessing the argument than her threat to walk back to London. 'You're insane, Andrew.'

'Better that than walking back to the city,' he replied with a cold and calculating smile. 'I will leave you here if you don't get back in the car immediately.'

As if she cared right now. She wasn't some big city woman who had never had to walk a couple of miles before. He might not remember the details she had told him about her life, but it didn't stop her from being a country girl. She'd spent years walking around the lake back home. 'You have no idea just how little your threat or any words from you mean to me right now. Andrew. I've already made it clear that I am quite prepared to walk home or to the nearest train station if I have to. I'll hitchhike back to London and share a cab with a four hundred pound trucker who hasn't washed in a month if it means avoiding you.' She turned, stalking away from the sound of the car.

'I'm the best thing to ever walk into your life!' he yelled through the car window. 'This isn't one of your stupid novels, Anita. There's no knight in shining armor waiting around the corner to rescue you. No fair prince to sweep you off your feet. Your choices are simple ones, get back in my car or face a bloody long walk down to Kendal,' he yelled, then swore as she continued to walk away. He gunned the engine into life as the car turned behind her. For a brief moment she almost thought he would run her over and leave her bleeding by the wayside, but that was just her imagination getting the better of her. However mad Andrew was with her, he wasn't the type to try and kill her, though that didn't stop her from feeling relieved as she heard his car pull away.

The long and narrow lane snaked out in front of her as she shouldered her small bag. Well, the last sign had mentioned a town only four miles away, it wouldn't take that long to walk to it, and if she was lucky someone would stop to give her a ride. Once In town she might be able to find a way back to London. It was all simple enough, as long as she kept calm, then she would pack. After the way Andrew had reacted there was no way she was ever planning on speaking to him again. How could she have ever been so blind as to not see his temper, or realize just what he thought of her writing?

Scribbles indeed. How many times had she heard her work called that or some other mocking term by people who didn't understand what it was like to love writing the way she did? Just once it would have been nice to meet a man who didn't look down on her career as if it was nothing more than a meaningless hobby. She sighed, rubbing at her shoulder before looking down the road towards vague signs of humanity. 'It's just a light stroll, be over and done with in an hour or two.'

In low-heeled shoes and comfortable jeans, Anita began the long walk down the unfamiliar road towards the town…

* * *

Her feet burned as she slipped the shoes off, every muscle in her body screamed a protest at the length of the day, the walking, the hiking through unfamiliar countryside, waiting two hours for the train only to be forced to endure a five hour train trip in a rattling carriage with uncomfortable plastic seats. Getting something to eat had been a nightmare; she hadn't been willing to explore, not after one look at the plastic-wrapped sandwiches on sale at the train station. She had risked the coffee, but nothing else, and even that had been almost too foul for her to finish. It must have been that instant coffee so popular in England. Very few places stocked the good filter coffee she was used to, and expecting to find coffee in a station diner had been too much to hope for. It was just one more reason why she needed to go home. At least now she understood the local jokes about British rail food.

She slumped down into the love seat, rubbing at her aching feet. As much as she wanted to slink into a good hot bath right now, the thought of even walking those last few steps to the bathroom filled her with ennui. She was out of condition for walking long stretches, and her shoes hadn't been bought with the thought of walking more than a mile in them. The only highlight of the trip back into the city had been the long-haired man with light-blue eyes that had sat opposite her for an hour of the trip. He had smiled only a handful of times during the journey, lost in whatever music had been playing on in his earphones. Had he been English or of Nordic descent? Perhaps a combination of the two; there was no way of telling and they hadn't even shared a 'hello', but his appearance had been enough to spark a few ideas for possible characters. Or at least he would have done if the thought of writing hadn't sent sharp protesting winces running through her arms.

Kendal… what little she had seen of the town had been a beautiful place, a place that would have been an ideal setting for a Gothic romance. Most of what she had seen of England would also have fallen into that category. She hadn't had the chance to visit Scotland, and now with time running out it wasn't a possibility, not on this trip, at least. Perhaps in a few years time she would be able to return. That was if she ever managed to rid herself of the foul taste lingering in her mouth which Andrew had become. Bad taste or not, she would have to visit again soon if only to investigate for herself just what men wore under their kilts.

The plane tickets still sat in full view on her mantelpiece as she looked around the apartment for any signs that Andrew had been here before she arrived. Nothing seemed out of place and she had put the chain on the door to be on the safe side after locking it behind her. Even as angry as he had been she couldn't see him trying to break in; he wasn't that sort of man. Then again until today she had never expected him to lay demands on her about her writing and by doing so totally ignoring the things she enjoyed in life.

Insane man. She would never demand or even suggest that someone give up their dreams for her. How dare he think she would do that for him? He would barely give up a late Friday evening at work without a scowl and a lot of persuasion. Well the matter was over and done with as far as she was concerned.

A slow blinking light on her answering machine caught her gaze. Only a handful of people had her number, and she knew without even checking that it would be Andrew. Her Editor had called two days ago and wasn't due to check in again for another week, just before she was due to fly home. Her Uncle was about the only other person likely to call, and he normally called on the cell phone, unless he had actually managed to remember to program her new number it. She loved her Uncle, he was the only remaining member of her family even if she didn't see him that often these day, but she was the first to admit just how forgetful he could be.

Whoever it was, they could wait until after her bath, which, if she didn't start moving for it now, would also wait until the following morning, and for that she would pay dearly. She winced with every step of the way as she pushed herself up from the love seat and hobbled towards the bathroom, muttering some choice words under her breath.

Thirty minutes later the aches in her body didn't seem to matter quite so much. Warm water caressed her skin, lapping between her thighs as she rested her head back against the waterproof bath pillow. Lavender and Chamomile both mingled in the swirling waters of the whirlpool bath, sending soft bubbles dancing along her thighs, smoothing across her belly to form cups under her bobbing breasts.

The bubbles moved beneath her fingers, smoothing across her skin as she spread them to form playful peaks on each ripe nipple, teasing the skin beneath with her fingertips. Andrew never shared the tub with her, and he had made it very clear that he looked on it as a childish waste of money, something she didn't need or he was unwilling to understand. Not that she would have offered him time in the tub with her to begin with. This was her place, her time, not something to share with him or any other man.

She could be wicked in the water, relax in the embrace of warm bubbles as she explored her body with her own fingers. If she hadn't been so angry at what the day's events had brought she would have allowed herself the luxury of that touch now. No, she wasn't going to take something she enjoyed and turn it into a way to push him from her mind. Even then it was tempting to let her fingers dip between her thighs and tease them across the hidden nub of her clitoris. Would it be so wrong to relax into the languid wickedness of her own fingers, to let them part the lips of her labia and allow the warm water to press into her sex?

No, with the mood she was in even her own touch would turn sour and she'd end up in a foul temper. Right now she was sore, but at least able to relax. Finding an apartment with this bathtub had cost her extra, but she had grown used to a hot tub and the thought of going even a week without a soak in the tingling bubbles had been something she had been unwilling to face. Not when she needed to be able to relax in order to write. But even this hadn't helped release her stubborn muse. London was a wonderful city, filled with people that should have been the source of a thousand stories, yet it had only shown her one thing – she belonged by the side of her lake.

It was time to go home.

Chapter Three

'Anita, if you get this call before six o'clock will you call back? Seems an old friend of yours is in town.' The familiar voice of Mark, the owner of the *Darvin Daily Paper* sounded out from the answering machine. Now there was a man she wouldn't mind enjoying the occasional savage fuck with if he could be trusted to lose his obsessive streak. She had seen that come into play more than once with girlfriends of his over the years, and though he had the type of looks that evoked a deep clenching in her cunt, she had no desire to be the next love of his life. Because of that she avoided him sexually, even to the point of keeping him at arm's length when he tried to kiss her at a local wedding. Still, his voice was a welcome one to come home to even if it was just on the machine.

She hadn't been home long; her bags still sat by the front door as she listened to the messages from her familiar machine. Maybe it was a little old fashioned to use an answering machine instead of a message service, but she preferred them. After her stay in London the lack of noise beyond the small house was a welcome relief. Looking back, she knew she hadn't really noticed the sounds or smells of the city until they were no longer a part of her morning routine. Now she welcomed the quiet and looked forward to her first night's sleep in her own bed.

An old friend? Well, whoever it had been was long gone by now; the message was a good month old. Not that she had the time to go out or the energy, what with the ten hour flight and the time difference; her body just wanted to crash. If she was lucky she'd get the chance to unpack her bathroom bag before falling into bed.

The last few days in London had been a blur of packing and getting the apartment ready to leave. She had moved out within three days and spent a couple of nights in a hotel rather than face the possibility of Andrew knocking at her door. He had tried apologizing, flowers, chocolates, and offers of a face-to-face apology, but in all honesty she had been relieved to know the truth of his nature before she made any rash decisions to stay in England. Had she come close to giving up her home for him?

That was a question she had faced time and again since her train trip back to London. Each time she had wanted to say 'no' only to find that the answer was 'maybe', 'possibly', with the right question aimed her way. If he had asked her to marry him then it would have been more than 'maybe'. She'd had a near miss, she understood that now, though it didn't make her feel any better. Marrying him would have been the worst mistake of her life. Ridiculous, the whole situation was beyond being ridiculous. She had her home, her writing, and in most cases her choice of men when she was looking for a date, so allowing herself to become so wrapped up in a daydream about a man she would now sooner never see again was beyond her.

He hadn't given up on her completely, despite her hopes that he had. The argument he had tried to force in *Heathrow Airport* had been a scene worthy of a soap opera. Between his yelling, and the onlookers that had tried to alternatively cheer him on or tell him to leave her alone, she had been left wanting nothing more than to sink into the floor. The saving grace had come in the form of the heavily armed airport policeman who had escorted him from the premises as soon as it had been made clear that she was trying to travel home and wanted nothing to do with him. He had actually helped there by losing his temper and yelling at the police officer, demanding to speak to his superior. It had seemed even in England that sort of attitude didn't go over too well with the police or security. The last time she had seen Andrew, he was being escorted out of the airport and towards a waiting car. She might have joined him if she hadn't remained calm despite every hurtful word he had thrown at her, and the fact that she didn't hesitate to show her ticket to a female officer. The strange part had been that the woman had recognized her name and asked her for a quick autograph as soon as her colleagues were out of hearing range. That had been a strange ending to a very tense morning.

'Foolish,' she muttered as she grabbed the smallest of the bags and carried it through into her bedroom as the rest of the messages played through. 'Whoever does marry that man will be sorry.' She dropped the suitcase down on her bed and began searching through it for her bathroom bag. She'd had a near miss, and it was best left at that, or at least that was what she finally decided as she found the pale lavender bag buried beneath two t-shirts and a satin nightshirt. Within a few days she'd have recovered from the trip and be ready to slip back into her life by the side of the lake.

How could she have ever considered leaving the lake in the first place? Just the short drive back home had reminded her of the beauty of the place. The herons strutting along the bank had even called out their greeting as she had hauled her luggage from the car.

'Anita, I hope you don't mind me giving you a call…'

Where Mark's voice had sent a tight clenching through her sex, Craig's voice released memories that caused her skin to tingle as her thighs pressed tightly together. 'I managed to persuade Mark to pass your number on to me, though he made it clear you were out of town on business…'

The voice coming from the machine caused her breath to catch in her throat.

'Well, I'm not sure when you'll be back, but when you do get this message, look me up. I'm going to be staying out at my parents' old place. Well, guess it's mine now. I'm rambling, sorry. Anyway, I'm back for good and I hoped we could at least meet up for a drink, a meal, a coffee... I've missed you, Anita.' There was a moment's silence as if he was gathering his thoughts before continuing. 'It's Craig, Craig Dawson, by the way, silly huh, almost didn't think you might not remember my voice. Well catch up with you soon, or hope to.'

Craig Dawson. How many years had it been since she had seen or heard from him? Five, six? It had to be about that by now. He'd left town not long after her twenty-first birthday. What had the argument been about? The fight had left her in tears, and refusing to leave her house for close to three weeks. He'd wanted her to leave town with him, but her reluctance to leave the area had been the trigger, though now she couldn't remember just exactly what remark had sent her running for cover. Whatever it had been, it was in the past, and now he was back home. Even better than that, he wanted to meet up with her.

Craig was a man she might have been willing to give up almost anything for, not her writing, however, and not her home, but anything else. Well, almost anything else. For those ice-blue eyes she had almost been willing to give up her soul, and she had given up something else, too...

Heat flushed across her cheeks at the memory of that single night on the beach so many years ago. He hadn't realized he was her first until the moment his cock had pushed deep into her tight sex and torn through the barrier she had wanted him to break from the moment she had been old enough to understand sex. She hadn't been the only one with a crush on him; half the girls in her school had watched his every move with a look that bordered on blind hunger.

Had he known that? He would have had to be blind not to notice, but she was now well aware of just how blind both men and women could be to the reactions they caused.

Men… they always wanted her to leave her home. Well she wasn't about to go tracking him down any time soon. All she wanted to do was have a shower, grab something to eat and crawl into bed while she could still see clearly enough to hit the pillows with memories of Craig pushing their way to the surface as a welcome replacement for the man she had left behind in England.

Craig had gentle hands that could find the most sensitive spots on her tingling skin, she remembered that much about their one evening together, gentle hands and a seeking mouth. Between the two she had arched up towards his body, clawing into his arms to hold him tight to her. Even when young he had worked out, but not in a gym; honest work, as she preferred to call it, kept him fit. A construction company was the family business. Did he still work out?

Her fingers drifted down over her breasts, cupping them as she parted her thighs, rocking her hips upwards at the thought of his tongue lapping over her throbbing clit. He'd caressed her thighs as his head pressed between them, taking her clitoris in his mouth and letting her ease back onto the clean sand at the edge of the water. He'd had more experience than she had claimed, but that wouldn't have been hard considering he had been her first. Time had lost meaning beneath his caresses and his light kisses had left her body crying out for something she hadn't even understood at the time. Even the brief pain as his cock thrust into her tight yet eager pussy had been welcome. They had slept together only that once, but she had replayed the delights of that night over and over in her mind more times than she could count. His eyes... she had been able to let her dreams drift within them any time his gaze had met and held her own... but that was so long ago now that all she dared hope for was the memory to remain one she could lose herself in on nights like this. Here in her bedroom she could enjoy his touch in her dreams even if though she doubted she'd get the chance to relax into his arms again in real life. They hadn't spoken since he left town so many years ago, so the thought of somehow slipping back into a relationship with him was beyond foolish. He was more than likely married with two kids and had a happy life without her.

Yet still her body shivered and her dreams clung to the memory of being with him as sleep finally claimed her for the night.

* * *

'Anita? You awake in there?' an all too bright voice called out, tugging her from the warmth of sleep. 'Come on, sleepy head, you got back in last night, don't tell me you're still in bed.'

The door of her bedroom creaked open as her eyes opened enough to focus on the figure holding a covered basket. The stimulating smell of rich coffee filtered into her groggy senses.

'Lynn? Is that you?' she queried as she tried to sit up, but the white sheets were tangled about her legs. For a moment she was uncertain just who it was that had walked into her home so early in the morning. It had to be early or she wouldn't still be sleeping. She grasped the edge of the sheets, holding them over her naked breasts. 'Lynn?' she repeated, blinking the sleep out of her eyes.

'Well who else has a key? I told you I'd keep an eye on your place while you were away, remember?' Far too much energy for early morning smiled back at her from a set of deep-brown eyes and matching bangs. 'I've brought you some muffins as I didn't think you'd be in the mood to go anywhere just yet, and I've got the coffee on.'

'I can smell it.' She pushed slowly up onto her elbows as she spoke, still trying to blink the jetlagged sleep from her eyes. 'Isn't it a little early for this?'

'Early? Anita, it's nearly three o'clock,' Lynn replied with a grin. 'Guess you slept longer than you realized. Heard jet-lag can do that to a person.' She sat down on the edge of the bed, uncovering the basket before setting it on the bedside table. 'I've got so much to tell you, but I guess you need to wake up a little more. Maybe shower, grab some coffee. You never were much good before your first cup.'

'Three? As in three o'clock in the afternoon?' She glanced towards the clock. 'I didn't plan on sleeping in. Guess I forgot to set the alarm.'

'Or you turned it off.' Lynn replied with a shrug. 'No harm done, you wouldn't have slept that long if you hadn't needed it. But if you want that coffee fresh you might want to think about getting out of bed, unless you plan on spending the day in there.'

'I'll be up in a few, I just need a little privacy first.' She yawned and looked at her friend. Lynn was a good woman, but there were times you had to be blunt with her or she wouldn't take the hint.

'Privacy?' Lynn blinked and grabbed the basket of muffins as she looked at Anita in confusion before a blush flared over her face. 'Oh!'

'I need to get dressed. So out you go. Go on!' She ushered the other woman out with a wave of her hand and a soft laugh, only grabbing for her robe once the door was closed. At least her friend was someone she could joke with. Damn, but she was still sleepy. Lynn was right, she wouldn't have slept so long unless she'd really needed to, although she did feel a little foolish for not setting the alarm. Still, it wasn't as if she had any plans for the day.

The coffee smelled great, and with a pair of jeans and a loose fitting sweatshirt in place, she headed out to the kitchen and her waiting friend. 'I owe you for this, Lynn, my fridge is bare.' She eased onto one of the stools at the breakfast bar. Her day and her smile both brightened at the sight of the single white rose rising from a slender vase on the counter along with a card that simply said *Welcome Home*. The kitchen was one of the largest rooms in the house, a holdover from when it had been the center of life for her family and the four generations that had come before. A large table sat at one end of the kitchen, although eating alone Anita normally used the breakfast bar, one of the new additions, or she took her meals out on the deck when the weather was nice.

'You do owe me,' Lynn agreed complacently. 'I picked some stuff up for you yesterday morning, including a loaf of bread, some coffee, cheese, yogurt, bacon and eggs. I didn't think you'd be up to shopping yet, but I wasn't sure if I'd make it out here this morning either. This way I knew you'd have something around to eat when you got up. Then I remembered this morning that you wouldn't know about the food and wouldn't be up to going anywhere for a few hours after you woke up, so I got dressed, went into town and hurried back here.'

'How much did I pay you for the housekeeping service again?' Anita reached for the coffee mug as Lynn pushed it her way.

'You didn't.'

'That's something I need to change.' The coffee tasted as good as it smelled. 'I didn't realize just how much I'd missed a good coffee until now. The stuff they have in England isn't bad as long as you make sure they're serving you filter and not that instant stuff.'

'No, you don't need to do anything to change the situation, Anita, we've had this discussion before. You're a friend and this is what friends do for each other, remember?' Lynn smiled as she spoke, firmly. 'You'd barely remember to eat some weeks if you didn't have me stopping by.'

'That's true, and all the more reason I should pay you for that.' When a story hit she could forget what day of the week it was. That had happened more than once, but the first time Lynn found out she had stepped into the role of caretaker and housekeeper for her muse-trapped friend.

'First read through of the stories you write, you know that's all I'll ever ask for,' Lynn insisted.

'I don't think it could ever be enough. Not when you go to all this trouble for me. Between the food you make sure I'm eating, reading through my work, companionship, and the way you keep an eye on my home while I'm away, and now this rose, it's wonderful.' She reached out to cup the delicate petals.

'I didn't get you the rose, it was delivered this morning along with the card. I just assumed it was a welcome home from Sue.'

'It's pretty whoever it's from.' She picked up the card, looking over it before setting it back down on the counter. 'Well, it might be from Sue, if so she forgot to sign it.'

Lynn set her mug down on the counter, meeting her friend's eyes calmly. 'How did it go, in London, I mean? Something happened there, I know that much and I'm betting it had to do with a man. One day you were fine, happy, talking about extending your visit, the next I get a call saying you're coming home.'

'It's a long story.' She tried avoiding it the easy way.

'I'm not going anywhere.' Lynn smiled warmly. 'At least not until you tell me what happened.'

'Are you going to let this drop?' she asked hopefully, already knowing the answer.

'Only after you've told me what happened.'

'Fine.' She took a mouthful of coffee, then set the mug down on the counter, giving herself time to formulate her story. 'Well, if you want to know about Andrew, I'd best get that over and done with so I can move on.'

'That might be an idea,' Lynn pushed.

Reluctantly, and over two more cups of coffee, Anita explained what had happened between her and Andrew. By the time the story was finished Lynn had resorted to swearing, and that was with the sanitized version of the story. As much as she and Lynn were friends, she couldn't bring herself to explain about going down on her hands and knees. What she did cover about the sex still had her blushing deeply.

'That bastard! I can't believe he just expected you to stop writing and leave home for him. Why? What happened between you two that was so wonderful he assumed you'd drop your world for him just because you and he screwed a couple of times? He doesn't sound like he was that good in bed to begin with.' Lynn shook her head as she slipped down from the kitchen stool.

'Something along those lines, yes.' Anita also slipped down from the stool and gave her friend a quick hug, grateful she hadn't gone into details with her. Perhaps Lynn would just assume the heat she could feel radiating across her cheeks was just from anger recalling the situation. 'It's over and done with now, he's not a part of my life anymore and never will be again.'

'Now correct me if I am wrong, but that would be Anita-speak for "drop the topic and never mention it again"?'

'Exactly.' The sooner Andrew was a faint and distant memory, the better. Now she was home and there were far more important things she could focus on. She had her work, the lake, unpacking, settling back into life in general, and a dozen other things to fill her time. 'So, how about we start with you helping me catch up on what's been happening while I've been away.'

Lynn's laughter filled the small kitchen as she linked one arm through that of her friend and tugged her out towards the deck. 'Oh, more than you can imagine, Anita. You wouldn't believe some of the interesting people who've suddenly come to town. On top of that, there's some building work being planned. Half the town is up in arms about it.'

As the two women walked out onto the deck, a flock of herons flew low over the lake which bore the name of the occasional cranes that frequented the place, their feet trailing over the surface of the sun-touched water. She had missed this, the quiet beauty of the light reflecting back from the small waves as the birds stalked their way through the long reeds. 'There's always building work going on somewhere, Lynn.'

'Not like this. You'll see for yourself at the meeting. I should have sent you the papers while you were away, they've been running some good articles about the situation although Mark has been his usual scathing self about the plans, not surprising, though, considering what the company wants to do with the land. But I'm sure Connor still has your copies of the paper along with the rest of your mail. It should make for some interesting reading.'

Anita turned, giving her friend a hard look. 'What's being going on, Lynn?'

'It would be better you caught up with the information

yourself, that way you'll come to it with a clear set of eyes. Isn't that what you always told me was the best way to work, to gather information without anyone else's thoughts clouding your judgment?' Lynn replied, but she avoided her friend's eyes as she spoke. 'No matter which side of the argument you side with, it's not going to be a pretty situation.'

* * *

'How was London?' Connor smiled from the other side of the counter.

Anita had only just made it to the post office in time, barely five minutes before the door was locked, but Connor seemed in no hurry to chase her out. The older man had run the local post office for the past ten years and knew everyone in the area, even if only by the periodicals they had delivered.

'Was it as foggy as they show in the movies? Did it rain a lot?'

'No, it was nothing like that at all. Nice weather most of the time, a few bad days, but that was about it. Still, I'm glad to be home. I've heard there have been more than a few changes recently, some building work planned?' she inquired as she sorted through the mail that had backed up during her time away. Packages lay next to bills and junk mail as she tried cutting down some of the correspondence she'd have to take back home. Out of everything that had accumulated over the months she had been away only ten envelopes, a pile of newspapers, and two packages seemed to be worth her time to carry home. Small town or not, she would keep the papers to read through over the coming weeks, using them as a way to catch up with friends and local events. She'd had the chance to work for Mark and the local paper, but it had never felt right to take up the offer, not when she knew he'd probably expect her to become his girlfriend judging by the time he had bent her over one of the desks in his office.

It wasn't vanity to presume he would try to take advantage of her working that closely with him, it was simply his nature. She wasn't unattractive, and he'd made his interest in her very obvious each time they met. The last time she had been offered the position had been right before her trip overseas. Mark had tried with soft words, teasing touches and wine to persuade her to work with him, and she had left with a promise that she would give it her full consideration when she returned home. Only now, looking over the newspapers, did she recall the promise made. If she could persuade him that anything that happened between them didn't constitute a commitment, then the job might be just what she needed right now.

'There's to be a meeting at the town hall about those plans on Saturday evening,' Connor informed her, breaking into her thoughts. 'I expect you'll be there.' He pushed a form in front of her so she could sign for her mail. 'Or are you still recovering from the flight?'

'A meeting?' She looked up from the papers. 'Oh, right, the planning committee?' She signed the form.

'The second stage meeting, yes.' He took the signed form back from her, filing it away. 'Those plans have caused more than a few problems here, Anita. Not everyone likes them. Some people are all for them, and the work it might bring here, but I don't think the damage it would lead to is a good idea. I can't see you sitting back quietly and letting them tear up around the lake like that, either.'

Her throat dried out as disbelief filled her words, '*My* lake? They're planning to build around *my* lake?'

'Yes, it's right here in last month's special edition.' He reached for the papers in front of her, searching through them until he found the yellow colored special. There, on the front page, in clear black print, was a copy of the proposed construction plans around the lake – houses, a boat dock, a small hotel, even a golf, course were all clearly mapped out around the edges of *Lake Crane*. 'See, there's your house.' He pointed out the small set of box-like markings that indicated her house and barn. 'You really didn't know about this?'

'No.' She'd wasted time talking about idiot boy back in England instead of finding out about the local news. The very idea of them disturbing the cranes, ruining the quiet she had come to cling to, put a knot into her stomach. She'd not come all the way home only to see that home destroyed. She tapped the plans with her fingers as she spoke, focusing for a moment on the name of the company. 'I'm not going to let this happen. If this *New Vision Construction* wants to dig up around my home they have a fight on their hands.'

'Now that is exactly what I was hoping you would say, Anita.' A tight smile and a glint in his eyes emphasized his words.

She was still fuming thirty minutes later when she stalked

back across the high street to her car. The more time she had to think about the plans emblazoned across the front page of the newspaper, the more furious she became. By the time she strode towards her car she was muttering curses beneath her breath, and so focused was she on what she would do if she met the person behind the plans that she didn't hear someone call out her name behind her. When a hand touched her shoulder just as she put the key into the lock of her car door, she literally jumped.

'What the hell do you think you're doing, grabbing a woman like that?' She turned, one fist clenching as she tried to calm her breathing down. She was met by a pair of deep-blue eyes and a confident smile that still had the power to make her weak in the knees. Jet-black hair curled under his ears, resting in loose waves over his shoulders before vanishing from sight down his back. She wasn't sure how long he wore it now, but he was one of the few men she had ever known who could carry off the long, wavy look without any effort at all. 'Craig?' she breathed.

'The one and only,' he replied, his hands grasping her arms as he looked her over. 'Damn but I swear you look even better than I remembered.'

'You look good yourself,' she said as she let her gaze linger on his body. 'Good' was an understatement; even beneath the denim shirt she could see the lines of his muscular chest. Did he still sport six-pack abs? Somehow she doubted he would have let that slide, not from what she could see of him. He didn't wear tight jeans, preferring (or so it seemed) to wear ones that were suited to easy movement, but even then she could tell his ass was just as tight as she recalled from high school days. What had changed was the air of confidence. Where once it had been a sham, something he had forced into place with time and practice, now it sat about him as a natural second skin. The boy had become a man, a man her body wanted to know far more about than he might be willing to permit. 'It's great to see you again, Craig.'

'Is that all I get?' An obviously fake pout settled over his lips. 'I've been gone for years and all you say is it's great to see me again? Don't I at least get a hug?'

She didn't need any further encouragement. She allowed his arms to encircle her body, pressing her close to his chest as she breathed in the scent she had come to know as his. That odd mixture of denim, *Drakkor Noir*, and his own sweat or musk, whatever you wanted to call it… it all combined into a smell she willingly breathed deeply of. She nuzzled closer to his neck, rising onto her toes as one hand caressed her back before grasping her ass with a firm squeeze. Her nipples hardened as she rested within his arms, a shiver working through her body at the memories his touch brought back to life. She could still remember how it felt to have his cock buried inside the tight walls of her virgin pussy.

His chin rested on her head, his voice rumbling through into her body as he spoke, 'Now you see, this is a lot better isn't it?'

'Not something I'll disagree with.' She could have stayed

within his arms for the rest of the day. 'Damn it, I've missed you, you barely even sent the occasional Christmas card, then in you walk large as life and you still have the ability to make me feel like I'm back in High School.'

'It's been more than a few years since then, hasn't it? I've been pretty busy, what with work and overseeing things for my parents. I was dashing all over the counties for a while with one job or the other. I don't think I spent more than a handful of nights in the same bed over the last two years. I know I should have made more of an effort to keep in touch, I've no excuse at all. But what about you? You're a big time author from what I hear, I even saw one or two of your books in the stores. Seems like all those days scribbling stories in the back of class instead of doing course work finally paid off. Some steamy stuff, a least from the one I had the chance to look over.'

'Oh, you've learned to read then?' she retorted.

The smack that cracked against her ass was more noise than pain, but it sent her pressing harder into his body even as the indignant protest formed on her lips. Her nipples hardened further, her cunt tightening even as she said, 'You arrogant bastard! What was that for?'

'That's easy enough to explain, Anita – because I can, and because you liked it a lot more than you're willing to admit.' He leaned down a little and pressed his lips to her neck. 'And don't tell me you didn't, not when I can feel the heat coming from you.'

She wanted more, needed more, but he'd been gone so long, and Andrew had been right about one thing, she wrote fiction, she didn't live in it. 'Don't,' she protested, pressing her hands against his chest and pushing away from his grasp. 'You can't just walk back into town and pull me into your arms as if we were still dating.'

'And are you going to explain just why not?' He took a step closer to her. 'It's not as if you didn't enjoy it.'

'Because it's not a polite thing to do.' She watched him raise an eyebrow at the word 'polite'. He was right, even if she didn't approve of what he had done, she hadn't wanted to leave his arms. 'And because I have things to do right now. Plus it's the middle of the day and the high street with people all around us.' There *were* people now, and more than a few had been staring at them.

Craig shrugged as he glanced around them, his gaze moving over the assembled men and women who had stopped for the momentary show.

Was it her imagination or did more than one of the people who suddenly went on their way look at him with hatred or anger in their eyes?

'Well, then, if not now, how about Friday night?' he asked. 'Say eight o'clock? I'll meet you on the beach and we can catch up then. I have a little work of my own to do as well, but I should have it all dealt with by then. I really would like to catch up with you again, and I can't think of a better place to do it.'

The beach... somehow the idea of meeting him there again pushed away any thoughts of protesting. 'Eight o'clock it is, and try not to be late this time.'

'This time?'

'Yes, the last time you met me there you were nearly an hour late, and this time I won't hang around for you.' She got into her car and opened the window, setting her mail on the passenger seat.

'Oh, I think you might,' he replied as leaned into the car.

'I wouldn't bet on it, Craig. I'm not that eager young girl anymore.'

'No, you're certainly no girl any more, Anita. You've become a strikingly beautiful woman instead, one that I hope will wait for me if I am a few minutes late.'

Chapter Four

'He's late, that son of a bitch is over thirty minutes late, and I'm still waiting for him!' she hissed as she paced along the beach, kicking at small clumps of sand. The days had flown past in a blur of unpacking, dropping into bed in an exhausted state only to wake up at odd hours during the day. She'd barely even had time to look over any information on the work that had been planned around the lake. However, that hadn't prevented her from noticing the men who had been periodically visiting the lake, measuring out sections of land nearby. It had taken every ounce of self control she possessed not to march over to them and demand they leave. If they thought she and the rest of the town were just going to sit back and let them destroy the area, they were insane. Now she waited for Craig to arrive, and was left pacing along the edge of the lake they wanted to ruin.

She had arrived early, even started a fire, laid down two blankets, and tied a string to a six-pack before lowering it into the edge of the lake so the beer would remain cold. And now she fought herself with every step along the edge of the water. He'd been so smug about her waiting for him and she wasn't sure what was worse, the fact she had waited or the fact he knew she would.

'Five more minutes, just five more minutes and I'm going back to the house and he can just go to hell for all I care.' Just like that first night they had been together she was torn in two between leaving and waiting for him. Even with so many years apart the craving to spend time with him was as strong as it had been before they parted with angry words. How could someone she had cried herself to sleep over, even sworn never to speak to again, have the ability to walk back into her life and reduce her to a nervous teenager again? And after nothing more than a short embrace in the middle of the street?

Well, regardless of whether he turned up or not, he had given her a reason to spend time walking along the edge of the lake. The plans she had seen in the newspaper flashed through her mind again. Anger mixed with the determination that, no matter what it took, she would not permit them to ruin the place that was her sanctuary.

Something had startled the cranes from the far side of the lake, sending them soaring across the surface of the water.

Sunlight reflected off their white outspread wings as they sought a quieter or a safer spot to rest. She had never understood why a lake that was home to both herons and cranes had been named after only one of the birds.

'I knew you'd still be waiting for me.' Craig's voice carried across the short span of the beach with little effort. 'A fire and blankets... nice cozy little set up you have here.'

'You haven't changed a bit,' she retorted, turning quickly to face him. He was smiling despite the annoyance in her voice, and the light breeze played through his hair in the same way she remembered. He wasn't wearing the same clothes he had been all those years ago, but the sight of him still caused her heart to skip a beat as she pressed her thighs tightly together. 'Ever thought I just decided to watch the birds for a little while and you never entered the picture?'

'No.' He grinned as he closed the distance between them with a few easy steps. 'If you hadn't set up all of this then maybe I might have been convinced? Then again, I doubt it.'

'Oh, that's it! You can enjoy the beach by yourself.' Anger outweighed her desire to spend time with him and she turned to stalk across the sand towards her home. 'You're just as arrogant as you were back in school. I should never have agreed to meet you out here.'

He caught her arm, turning her back to face him. 'Anita, there's no need for you to storm off like this.'

'I have every reason to. I'm not some love struck teenager anymore, Craig, you can't just keep me waiting and then act as if you own the place when you do finally deign to turn up.' She tried to pull her arm from his grasp. It didn't matter that she wanted to press herself into his arms and forget the years that had passed them both by; he was still the same self-assured bastard he'd been back then and she'd had her fill of men like him.

'I never claimed you were a love struck teenager,' he protested.

'Not in so many words, but you're certainly acting as though I am,' she snapped back at him, finally tugging her arm free. 'And I'm not about to waste my evening with someone who can't even apologize for being late.' She turned, avoiding his eyes, and began walking back towards her house.

'I'm sorry,' he offered as he hurried to catch up with her. 'Anita, wait. I really am sorry. I had planned to be here on time, it's just that the phone rang as I was heading out and, like a fool, I answered it. By the time I got off the call it was already gone eight and I came straight here.'

She turned to face him again, her hands planted firmly on her hips. 'And why couldn't you just have said that in the first place instead of doing the big smug routine?'

'Because I'm male and therefore an asshole at the best of times,' he explained. 'I would have thought you'd know how men are by now. You do make a living writing about them.'

'No, I write about dream men, Craig. The sort of men that most women want to spend the rest of their lives with but know they'll never get the chance as those type of men don't exist outside romance novels and movies.' The sort of man she had allowed her dreams to turn him into if she was going to be honest with herself. 'Women want a mix of rogue and asshole, combined with just enough gentleman to keep the asshole side from becoming overwhelming. So that's what I give them, men who aren't that noble but can still sweep the heroine off their feet and leave them breathless as they wait for more.'

'Is that what you want in a man?' He stepped closer and tipped her face upwards with a soft touch of his fingertips. 'A dream man?'

'No, of course not, I write those books but I don't live in fantasy novels,' she retorted. 'I want a man who's real, faults and all, one who can accept me for all that I am.' A man like him who sent tremors through her pussy every time she thought of him. 'I don't expect a perfect man, I've learned the hard way those don't exist. You were the first one to show me that very clearly.'

His jaw clenched. 'I'm not proud of how I treated you back then Anita.'

'You could have fooled me. The entire town knew before the end of the following day. I couldn't show my face in town for nearly a month because of you.' All the old bitterness came sweeping back. 'Just because I wouldn't up and follow you it didn't give you the right to turn me into the town whore.' He tried stepping closer to her, but she was too angry to let him, and before she knew what she was doing she had slapped both her hands against his chest in an effort to push him away.

'I never turned you into anything like that, Anita. The only person who knew was my father.' He refused to be pushed back from her. 'I'm sorry I stormed off on you, but I never spread rumors about town. So you can find someone else to blame for that one.'

'There was no one else who could have done it, unless you expect me to believe your father had something to do with it!'

'If you'd known the bastard the way I did then you'd have suspected him long before you suspected me. Ever wonder why I left town as soon as I could? It wasn't just because of offers of work; I needed to get away from him before I lost my temper one time too often. It didn't matter what I did, how many grade A's I brought home, how many headlines the team had or how hard I worked, he still treated me like I was less than dirt. I was never going to be good enough. He's the reason I left, not you.' A mixture of bitterness and regret rang in his voice, his eyes darkening as he discussed the past with her.

She wanted to believe him, but all her interactions with his father had been pleasant ones. He'd even tried to shelter her from some of the nasty comments that had been aimed her way. It just didn't make sense he would be the one responsible for the hurt she had suffered. He'd been a good man, a pillar of the community, so to hear that he'd treated Craig badly only added to her sense of unease. It wasn't easy for her to accept that his father could have been behind the hurt she had been subjected to. 'You can't expect me to believe that...'

'Why not, I mean, just think about it, Anita. How many of my games did he ever show up on time for? Did you ever see him at the after game party unless he was there to conduct business? Do you remember my eighteenth birthday party out at the *Red Deer*? He walked out within five minutes of arriving for the meal as he had a business meeting. Put the pieces together. All that time and money organizing it, my friends, family, even our teachers there, and it wasn't important enough to him to bother re-scheduling his meeting so he could stay.' He flung the information at her quickly, then shook his head. 'I don't know why I am bothering, no one will ever believe what he was really like, not even others he hurt just for his own amusement.' His hands had clenched at it sides, the anger and hurt in his voice causing it to crack slightly as he spoke. 'Forget it, I should never have tried to meet you out here. All I've managed to do it rehash some bitter memories for us both.'

'Bitter memories? What would you know about my memories? You have no idea what I went through when you left or how I used to feel about you. But go ahead, Craig, walk away, you've been doing that all your life, why change now.'

'What?' He turned, anger written across every muscle in his body.

'You walked away from the problems you had with your father and with me, walked out on the town, on friendships, on love. Now you're walking away again. Have you ever stood up for anything you really wanted in your life?' She took a step closer to him, lashing out at him with her accusations. 'Because if you have, I certainly haven't seen any evidence of it.'

'You've no idea what I've done with my life,' he answered

after taking a slow, deep breath. 'I've been places, actually done some things I'm proud of since I left this place.'

'Yet you're walking away from me again, walking out on me and any feelings I might have for you.'

'Just as you were ready to a few moments before,' he reminded her. 'Or are the rules different for women? I remember you walking away from more than a few challenges in life, and backing down to your mom just to keep the peace. And feelings, what feelings?'

She wanted to yell that what she had done was different and had nothing to do with the conversation, but he was right, perhaps more so than he even realized. 'Is there a point in discussing that with you right now? I'm not even sure if these feelings exist or if they're just emotions from when we were kids, but you're willing to walk away before either of us have the chance to find out.'

'So, Anita, are we just going to walk away from each other or are we going to enjoy the set up you have here and try and repair our friendship?' He took another deep breath before he reached for her hand, brushing his thumb over her knuckles for a moment as he waited for her answer.

The silence stretched out painfully as she tried to calm herself down enough to think clearly. They both had tempers, she'd always known that, but he'd offered the olive branch and she could only be woman enough to accept it. 'Where did you go after you left town?' she asked quietly as she curled her fingers into his. At least they had dropped the discussion about feelings for the moment. She didn't know if she felt something for the man he was now or if she was still in love with the man he had been before he left town. There was no way of knowing, not this soon after meeting him again.

He led her over to the blankets and they settled down on them before he spoke again. 'I've been here and there, Chicago for a while, spent a year in Denver, six months in Houston working one construction job after the other. Odd jobs here and there when I couldn't find someone to continue learning the trade from.'

'You make it sound as though there were endless things to learn.' She watched the firelight casting a glow over his face. 'One brick on top of another, isn't it?'

'That's a bit like saying all it takes to write a story is putting pen to paper,' he countered swiftly, but a good natured grin took the sting from his words. 'Didn't I read an interview you did a couple of years back where you defended writing as a real job? Something about having to learn to edit, do research and not allow too much of yourself to enter the characters you create?'

'So you've been following my career?' That she hadn't expected. 'Or is that just another coincidence?'

He shrugged. 'I'm not going to hide it. I've kept a close track on your books and work, Anita. I wasn't ready to contact you back then, but getting your books, reading the interviews, they all helped me realize what a jerk I'd been.'

'A jerk... I think that's putting things a little mildly but it's certainly a good start.' She let her gaze linger on his shirt. 'Construction you say, well its certainly kept you in shape.'

'I don't spend so much time on the sites these days. I

started my own business two years ago and it's taking off nicely. It's still a struggle sometimes trying to put the right bid in and still coming out on top.' He leaned back on his arms and she had to struggle not to let her gaze linger so obviously on the outline of his cock through his jeans, but it didn't help when she could feel the heat radiating from her cheeks.

'You did always say you wanted to be your own man.' She forced her contemplation back to his face and the deep blue of his eyes. That was almost a bigger mistake than watching his cock as the heat increased across her cheeks and spread down her neck. 'Good to hear you were able to follow that dream through.'

'You look a little flushed, Anita. Have you been sitting too close to the fire?' He smiled teasingly.

She opened her mouth to speak only to find she couldn't form a sentence.

'Nothing to say or are you lost in thought?'

She grabbed a handful of sand and threw it across the fire at him, laughing as it splattered over his chest. 'You can take *that* as my answer.'

He grinned and pushed to his feet, walking over to join her on the same blanket. 'Well if you're going to throw things at me it's going to be safer for me to sit right here, don't you think?' A protest died on her lips as he leaned closer. 'And I much prefer not having to shout over the fire to hold a conversation with you.'

He was wearing the *Drakkor Noir* again, just as he always did. The scent, the fire and the softness of the blankets all combined to push away her doubts as he slipped an arm around her shoulders and pulled her closer. 'So why did you want to meet me out here, Craig? Not to discuss the past or what's happened since then; we could have done that anywhere. Was there something else?'

'I thought maybe there was, but I don't want to make any presumptions with you.' He spoke through the strands of her hair as he nuzzled closer. 'I never stopped thinking about you. It didn't matter where I was, at the end of the day I went to sleep wishing you were with me.'

Her throat tightened at his words. 'Why did you wish that?' She wanted the answer to be something special, that she meant the world to him, that she was his one true love, but even as she hoped for that the quiet, sensible part of her mind slapped the idea down.

'Because I missed you, Anita. I do still care for you, that's never changed.' His lips pressed against the side of her neck. 'I'm not going to claim I love you, I'm not sure I even know what love feels like, but I've never stopped regretting leaving you behind.'

The touch of his lips was more than she could fight. 'I spent months crying myself to sleep over you leaving.' She turned on the blanket, leaning into his touch as she wrapped her arms about his body.

'I never thought about the pain I was causing you when I stormed off.' He trailed his fingers over the curve of her breast. 'That was selfish of me, I know that now.'

His light touches were maddening as they continued over her neck and breast. She tried arching into them, seeking to make the contact firmer, only to have him pull back again. 'I healed in time,' she whispered and leaned into him even harder, tipping her head back as she sought his lips.

'Are you sure this is what you want?' he spoke softly against her mouth. 'I don't want to rush you into something you aren't ready for, but I'd be lying if I said I didn't want to turn back time with you.'

'Yes, I want this, Craig…'

She barely had the chance to reply before his lips covered hers. The light pressure against the side of her breast quickly became a firm grasp covering her already hard nipple. She arched her back and welcomed the fact that he didn't pull away from her this time. Did he know just how much she had wanted to do this again? His tongue parted her lips, seeking within the warmth of her willing mouth, his fingers grasping her covered nipple, pinching lightly as he rolled it between his fingertips. His teeth caught her bottom lip, tugging at it as he pulled back from the kiss and looked down into her eyes.

'I've waited a long time to be able to do this with you again, Anita.' He pressed her down across the blanket, tugging at the buttons to open her loose-fitting blouse, popping them open one by one. 'I've dreamed of being able to touch you, to taste you and feel you lying next to me again.'

She couldn't answer him; her ability to speak had somehow been switched off for the time being. Instead she half sat up to slide her blouse off as his hands moved to her jeans. He pulled down the zipper impatiently and yanked them down over her hips as she helped him by kicking off her shoes. Her pussy clenched at the intensity of his gaze beneath which she lay wearing just her bra and panties.

'I'd be a fool to think there's been no one between that time on the beach and this night,' he went on quietly, 'but I want to forget that for now, forget that I ever left and just enjoy being with you again.'

She reached up, slipping her arms around his neck, pulling him down to meet her mouth once more. Her nipples stood out beneath the thin covering of cotton. His lips claimed hers, crushing them against her teeth as she moaned in delight. With a fevered need she tugged at his shirt, pulling it away from his body only to be rewarded by the sound of a seam tearing. His skin felt smooth under her fingertips, the bulge of his cock brushing against her inner thigh through his jeans. He growled against her lips, pushing his tongue into her mouth, his fingers tugging one of her bra caps down and playing over her nipple, pinching, twisting gently, making her gasp. A dozen thoughts raced through her mind. Was he married? Was he dating? Did she mean more to him than another passing moment on the sand? Would he run away again tomorrow?

When he moved his lips from hers down to her hard nipple she lost the ability to think. His tongue traced her aureole, then his teeth scraped its stiff peak as she reached between them and unzipped his jeans. His boxers followed suit with barely a moment's hesitation, allowing her access to the hard flesh of his aroused cock. When she curled her hands around his thick penis he groaned, his erection throbbing in her grasp as she tightened her fingers around it.

'You've become a lot more forward than you were,' he groaned around her nipple, suckling it.

'I don't hear you complaining,' she replied, humor giving her access to her voice once more as she kicked the jeans from his legs, her hand clenching and unclenching about his cock in time to the pulsing beat in her damp sex. She arched up against him, tightening her grip on his rigid penis, working her hand towards the tip as she rubbed her thumb over his glistening head.

'I'd have to be an idiot to complain!' The strap on her bra broke as he tugged it from her body with his teeth.

She whimpered, her panties clinging to the damp lips of her labia. She wanted him to strip them off, but he just moved to her other breast, licking around the tight nub, barely touching her skin. His free hand slipped between her thighs, brushing over the damp cloth, tracing her lips and her clit with an all too gentle touch.

'Tease!' she hissed, releasing her hold on his hard-on to desperately push her panties down her legs. 'Now, Craig, please. No more soft touches or nips, just fuck me now!'

He laughed against her breast as he pulled his hand from between her thighs. 'And what if I want to take it slow?' He grabbed both her wrists, pinning them in a gentle but firm hold against the blanket. 'A kiss here…' He brushed his lips over her cheek, tracing a path across her lips to her other cheek as she moaned. 'A nip there…' His teeth closed on the nape of her neck, scraping across her skin. 'A press right here…' He pushed between her willing thighs, the head of his cock brushing against her vulva.

'Bastard!' she gasped.

'Yes, and you love it.' He didn't let go of her wrists, but she knew she could pull free if she really wanted to; his hold on them was little more than a token and one she surrendered to despite her need to feel his cock stretching her open.

'Yes, I love it,' she confessed, her nipples pressed against his chest. 'God, I do!'

His cock slid down over her sex lips, parting them with a controlled push, just barely entering her.

She cried out, arching her back until she felt his cock edge a little further into her aching pussy. He wasn't pushing forward and she needed him desperately, needed him in a way she was too ashamed to voice. Her arms were pinned but her legs weren't. With a triumphant growl she arched upwards, wrapping her legs around his body, locking her ankles behind his ass and pulling it forward, clasping his erection with her eager cunt as he drove himself deep inside her.

'You're a wicked woman,' he breathed as she tightened her hold on his cock. 'A wicked and eager woman I've missed like hell!' His grip on her wrists fell away.

'Gods!' She cried out as he thrust hard and fast into her body, sustaining a violent pace that left her breathless as she tried to match his penetrations, her hips rocking upwards so his balls slapped against her as she locked her ankles behind his tight ass cheeks. The more she lifted up the faster he thrust into her, pushing into her clenching walls. 'Oh, yes, yes, fuck me!' she begged against his shoulder.

'I thought that I was!' He might have laughed if he'd had the breath.

Her fingers tangled in his hair as she pulled his mouth down to meet hers again, moaning. Each penetration propelled her body closer to the edge, until time had no meaning at all; until all she knew was his cock in her cunt and all the delights that went with it.

'Going... going to come...' he groaned.

She didn't have the words to tell him she was, too. A cry tore from her lips that was swallowed by his growl, her thighs tightening around his body as a hot ecstasy reverberated through her pelvis as she felt him come deep inside her...

* * *

The sun-warmed water washed about her body as she walked into the lake. Nowhere in her dreams had she imagined Craig would find her again. Even if she had dared to hope, her commonsense would have silenced the fantasy. Now he had found her again the touch of his lips was something she could still feel over her breasts and her neck. He'd become harder than she remembered. Time and experience had changed them both, but perhaps now there was a chance for them, a hope they could explore what anger had destroyed.

'Water looks inviting. Mind if I join you?' he called out, standing naked at the edge of the lake. The dying light played over the body she had clung to beside the fire.

'Come on in!' She splashed her hand into the water. He didn't wait for a second invitation. With a smooth run and jump he dove in beside her. Laughter came so easily to her lips now, all the weight of the previous months fading away even as he captured her and pulled her against him.

'Well what have I here? Could it be I've captured a water sprite all wet and willing for me to take?' His lips brushed along the side of her neck, his cock already hard again as it rested along her thigh.

'I thought you already had taken me.' She leaned against his chest. 'I am so glad you came home the same time as I did.'

'I've been home for a month or so now.' He let her go and pushed onto his back, floating for a moment. 'Only planned to stay for a short while, but some business came up.'

'What sort of business?' She swam a little closer.

'I'm in the construction game, remember?'

A lump formed in her throat at his words, the pieces of falling into place in a way she didn't want them to. '*New Vision Construction*?' she asked, hoping she would be wrong.

'Yes, that's my company, it's been doing really well this last year, so I thought I'd take on something a little more challenging and closer to home and-' If he had been planning on saying anything else the words died before gaining breath as she swam closer to him, planted her feet on the bottom of the lake, balled up her fist, and threw a punch at him; a punch he caught and blocked with ease.

'You're behind the plans to destroy my home?' she spat the accusation at him as she yanked her arm free and turned to swim back to shore.

'Destroy? Who said anything about destroying it? I plan

on bringing new life here, new jobs and homes.'

'I live here because of the herons and the peace, I don't live here in order to see construction crop up everywhere.' She stormed out of the lake and grabbed one of the blankets. 'How could you even think of doing such a thing?'

He stumbled after her. 'It's business, that's all it is to me.'

'Well it's not all it is to me, damn you, this is my home, I live here, I have to see the changes and see the place I love change into something else.' She didn't stop to look back at him. 'You've not changed, Craig, you don't give a damn about the consequences of your actions. You're still the same arrogant bastard you were before you left town. I had hoped you'd change, but you haven't.'

'What consequences?' He tried grabbing her arm as she hurried away. 'What the hell are you talking about?'

'Look around you, what do you think putting up houses, digging around the lake, will do?' She turned, spitting the words at him. 'I want nothing to do with you, not until you put a stop to your plans.'

'Are you insane?' he demanded as he stared at her in shock.

'No, but you are if you want to ruin this place just to earn some quick cash.' She'd had enough of men to last her a lifetime. Not one of them cared for anything but themselves.

'I'm not about to sacrifice a hard-earned contract just because some woman wants me to.' He reached for his jeans, pulling them on over his damp skin.

'Is that what I am to you, some woman?' She didn't stop

to grab her clothes, leaving her accusation ringing in his ears as she ran for the safety of her home. If he called out to her again she didn't hear it; not even when the rushes caught at her legs did she stop. Only when she locked the door behind her and sank to the floor did she allow the tears to fall as she wrapped her arms about her knees.

Something had to be wrong with her. Every man she fell for turned out to be nothing more than a selfish bastard, and she didn't find out until she had let him find satisfaction between her thighs. She'd been a fool not to realize Craig had been behind the construction plans, she'd known he was in the trade, she'd seen some of the looks the locals had given him, and yet she'd ignored it all.

Crying out 'Why me?' wouldn't solve anything, but she *could* try and stop him. Even if it never meant feeling his lips touch hers again she'd find a way to prevent him from damaging the lake. It wasn't as if she loved him or he loved her; she'd been nothing more than a convenient fuck to him and he to her, a way to wipe out the months in London and regain a little of her past.

So why did she feel as if someone had just tied a band about her chest and pulled it tight?

Chapter Five

Her throat felt like sandpaper as she rolled out of bed and stumbled towards the shower. Sleep had come unwillingly, leaving her to toss and turn until her sheets had become a tangled mess about her hips. Every time she had dared to close her eyes she had seen him, his eyes boring into hers. Her skin still tingled from his caresses as she leaned back against the shower wall. Even the slightest thought of him had her cunt clenching with longing. Her body didn't seem to care about the destructive plans he was a part of; for all she knew he was the driving force behind them. She had to find out if he was just a hired contractor or just a hired hand she could forgive (maybe) if he desperately needed the money. Yet she still would have expected him to try and find some other project to bring in the income he needed. But this – destroying the very area she loved – was beyond her. How could anyone who had grown up near the lake want to destroy it?

'I'm a bigger fool than I ever thought I was,' she muttered to herself as she let the shower hit her skin in stinging jolts. The needles of water only served as a further reminder of his touch, jarring her still sensitive nipples before trickling down across her belly to fall in soft tugs from her clitoris. Smoothing the soap over her skin only added to the ache in her nipples, to the subtle tremors in the muscles of her thighs. She couldn't remember a time when she had felt this way before after being with a man – a need so great that it continued over into the following day. Every kiss and touch seemed to linger on her skin, even his scent remained with her, which had to be her imagination. With the water washing away the last remaining grains of sand still clinging to her body there was no way it would leave behind the smell of his aftershave. Her fingers played across her breasts, teasing them as lightly as he had done, hoping to find some relief from the pressure building within her. She couldn't let him touch her again, but she couldn't deny the pleasure he had given her.

Anita was shaking by the time she stepped out of the shower wrapped in a long towel. Unless she found a way to relieve some of the pressure inside her she would be a wreck before the day was a few hours older. She had become so accustomed to seeking her own pleasure in between boyfriends that she had, at one point, become nearly addicted to masturbation and hadn't seen anything wrong with it. Nor did she now...

The towel fell to the floor, caressing a path down her legs as she crawled onto the still unmade bed, her damp hair tangling about her shoulders. Was it so wrong to use his image to enjoy herself with?

Her fingers slipped between her already parted thighs, sliding over the slick nub of her clit, and her thighs parted even wider to welcome her own intimate touch against her the lips of her sex. He had thrust so hard into her body, ramming into her as if she were the only woman in the world for him.... her fingers pushed into the slick confines of her pussy, and soon she was matching the swift pace with which he had taken her body on the beach. Her thumb brushed over her clit, her fingers pushing deeper into her body, her hips rocking up against the palm of her hand. He had pinched her nipples... her free hand cupped one of her breasts, her nails closing around one of her nipples teasing a soft cry from her lips that quickly changed to a gasp as the walls of her cunt tightened around her plunging fingers. With a low moan she arched her spine, her head tipping back. Was she a slut for wanting sex more and more with each passing year, or for learning to enjoy bringing pleasure to her own body? If the answer was 'Yes' she didn't care. She could feel him pressing against her body, pushing between her thighs, his cock thrusting into her slick hole. She could feel his touch, his lips, his breath, his fingers grasping her hips, raising them higher so he could thrust himself deeper and deeper inside her...

A cry of delight rose from between her lips, her fingertips tightening around her nipple as she brushed her thumb wildly over her tender clit, forcing herself higher and higher, rocking back and forth until she collapsed across the dampened sheets in a trembling heap.

Arrogant or not, the man still had his uses.

* * *

A second quick shower and a cup of coffee later, Anita settled down at the breakfast bar trying to sort through the mixture of emotions and thoughts troubling her. She wasn't about to sit back and let Craig run rampant over her home, but the question still remained about how to fight back. The town meeting that night might provide some answers, but this wasn't a situation she had tackled before. Except for the occasional article she had written during her early days of writing, she had stuck mainly to fiction. How did someone go about protesting land development? There had to be some way to find out. She had access to the internet, and once she felt a little more awake she would take advantage of that and begin looking through any help sites she could find. Other places had faced situations like this and some might have set up sites to rally support. She walked out onto the deck, hoping the fresh air would help her calm down, and there, on the railing, wrapped in pale pink tissue paper, was a single white rose. Her fingers were shaking when she picked it up, turning the delicate flower in her hands as she looked around for some sign of the person who had left it. Unwrapping the paper finally provided the answer she needed. The note had been folded around the stem, just a handful of carefully written words in a light blue ink:

I'm Sorry for being a jerk. Please forgive me.
I've missed you.
Love,
Craig

How had he remembered her love for white roses after so many years? Still cradling the bloom in her hand, she carried it back into the kitchen and added it to the other one she now suspected had also been sent by him. What would make him send a flower to welcome her home?

The ringing of the telephone roused her from her thoughts.

'Hello?'

'Anita, it's Mark. Are you free this afternoon? I thought it might be time you and I had a chat, especially with all the shit going on at the lake. I could really do with your help on this one.'

'Help in what way?'

'You've lived out there all your life, you have special interest in the area and can put some real heart into the fight. I need you in on this one, Anita. Will you come in and talk to me about this?'

'Yes, I'll come in. Two o'clock sound okay?' She needed to do a little more research on the plans before she sat down to talk to Mark or anyone else about the situation.

'Sounds good to me. Meet me at the office?'

'See you then.' By the time she put the phone down she was already working through her options. The DNR might be the way to go, but she couldn't be sure without looking at the plans again. With a fresh cup of coffee in hand, and the newspaper spread out on the counter, she began jotting down notes as the ideas began to form in her mind.

Herons weren't a protected breed, not that she knew of, neither were cranes, but she could check that out more clearly once she booted her computer back up. Were there any rare wild flowers in the area? There had to be someone locally who would know the answer. But regardless if the answer came from some small blossom half hidden in the reeds at the edge of the lake or a rare toad, she would find it. Working with Mark would provide some additional problems, but those she would face when they arose. There was no doubt in her mind that they would crop up sooner or later, that's just how Mark was, but she couldn't let that stop her now.

Craig would be at the meeting tonight...

She set the cup down on the counter as she headed for her computer. Why did she even care what he thought of her? He'd got what he'd wanted, so had she, and that was the end of the matter.

As her fingers flew over the keyboard, ideas took the place

of her concerns and she slipped willingly into the world of research.

* * *

A little before two o'clock found Anita heading into town, a note pad filled with ideas sat on the passenger seat of her car. The research had done a lot to help calm her down and had succeeded in pushing away the majority of her thoughts about Craig. Once she was done with her meeting with Mark, she planned to meet up with Lynn for a meal, perhaps catch up on some of the local opinions before heading to the town meeting. Although she lived barely ten miles from town she saw little point in driving home only to have to drive back in within a couple of hours.

The drive into town left her calm, at least until she parked the car and caught sight of a group of men standing on the corner. There were five of them in total, and Craig was among them. Perhaps she was imagining things, but as she got out of the car she was sure Craig looked her way. Before she could even lock the door the sound of their laughter reached her ears. Her grip tightened on the notebook as heat touched her cheeks. She was sure he'd told them what had happened the night before. She was a silly slut who had thought spreading her legs would get him to change his mind about his plans. Or maybe she was an easy lay he was recommending to his friends. Her knuckles were white as she walked towards the newspaper office. The very way they looked at her made her feel as if they could see through her jeans and t-shirt. Of course he wouldn't have kept his mouth shut, he hadn't as a teenager, why would he now? And to think she had come close to believing his lies about his father. What sort of man made up lies about his own dead father like that?

No... she had to start thinking clearly. Why would he apologize only to tell half his work crew about them? They had to be talking about something else and her arrival had just been a coincidence.

'Hey, Anita, glad you could make it.' Mark smiled as she walked into the office. 'How was the trip to London?'

'Not something I had plans to talk about, if you don't mind. I thought you wanted me here to discuss the lake.'

His jaw tightened. 'You're a bit snappy today, aren't you?' He gestured to the chair on the opposite side of his desk.

'I didn't sleep that well, sorry, I shouldn't have taken it out on you.' She offered a quick apology as she sat down. 'It's been a long couple of days.'

'I can well imagine.' He let his gaze linger openly on her breasts before pulling it back up to meet her eyes.

He hadn't changed, nor had she expected him to. He was the same good looking womanizer. She was the first to admit he could probably have nearly any local woman he wanted, between the position of power he had owning the local paper and his looks. Ice-blue eyes, shoulder length blond hair, and a smile that was both well practiced and charming at the same time. He wasn't a thin man, but he had spent time building up his form. He hadn't hit the bulky stage of bodybuilding, not yet, at least, though she could see where it wouldn't take much. 'So, how long have you known about the plans?' she asked him, opening up her notebook.

'A little over two months now and I've been trying to stop them the entire time. I'm not sure why they've targeted your lake, but the plans went from three new houses on the north shore to an entire community almost overnight.' He leaned back in his chair as he offered the information.

'*New Vision Construction*... I still can't believe Craig is behind all of this.' She had promised herself she wouldn't speak his name.

'Ah, so you know our old school chum is the head of that wonderful corporation? Good, saves problems later on. He's come a long way from local football hero. I firmly believe most of the town would prefer it if he moved on and took his big dreams elsewhere.'

'I heard there were a few that were backing his plans.'

'A few, yes... well, maybe more than a few, truth be told., mainly the new blood, those who didn't grow up here, a few hopeful souls looking forward to the money working on the building site might bring them. Half of them will drink the money away.' He reached into his desk and pulled out a set of the plans she had seen in smaller form in the Paper. 'If you look here... they're planning on building directly around your home, right up to the edge of your property. Given half the chance, I think they'd try and buy you out, move you out of their new patch of heaven.'

That she didn't doubt. 'What's this?' She tapped a red-marked building on the plans.

'That would be the meeting hall for the new township.' He glanced at her. 'They don't intend for this to be an extension of our town, but to be an independent township, own Paper, own sheriff, and their own town hall.'

Now it began to make a little more sense. Mark wasn't the philanthropic sort, but threatened with a new local Paper right on his doorstep, one he had no controlling factor in, he had reason to fight back.

'A whole new town right slap bang on your lake.'

'It will ruin everything. If they had just stuck to the first plan of adding a few houses that wouldn't have been so bad, what made them decide to put a whole town up?' That was part of the situation she didn't understand.

'I've no idea, they never bothered to share that information with me.' He smiled acidly as he rolled the plans back up. 'So, do I have your help on this? I'm not going to lie, I could do with your skills to help write up the reports, to put some real depth of emotion into the call to get this thing stopped in its tracks. Will you help me?'

'Yes,' she answered without hesitation. 'I'm already looking into possible aid from the DNR, and these things don't happen overnight, not unless some payments have been made that we don't know about.'

'That's one possible angle to look into,' he agreed, settling an intense gaze on her figure. 'The other is who's the backer. Craig has done well over the past few years but he doesn't strike me as someone who's earned enough money to finance this. He has to have help from somewhere. Whoever that is might not be aware of the public opinion out here.'

'Or he might have done far better than anyone has guessed.' She shifted in the chair. 'Mark, there's no need to look at me as if I'm a main course at a feast.'

He laughed, slapping his hands down on the edge of the desk. 'Why not, you look perfectly edible to me, Anita, and I am a very hungry man.'

'Mark,' she warned in a low voice, never taking her eyes off his.

'I'm just kidding. There's no need to get upset with me. I'm not going to hide that I find you just as attractive as I ever did, but I'll try not to be too offensive.'

'That sounds like it's going to be a strain for you.' She looked over the notes in her notebook. 'But as long as you keep your hands to yourself, and your mind on the work, then we shouldn't have a problem.'

'And what if I don't keep my hands to myself?' he asked, reaching out across the desk to catch her hand. 'What if I want to touch on occasions?'

She pulled her hand back. 'One warning Mark, that's all I'm giving you, one warning. I'm not here to play dodge around the desk with you, and if you can't accept that then I'll walk out now and find another way to fight Craig on this.'

His eyes hardened as he sat back. 'I see. Well, I can't say I like that idea so I'll keep my hands to myself unless you give me an indication you've changed your mind.'

It would be a cold day in hell before that happened, but instead of saying that she just smiled calmly. 'That sounds workable to me.' It would have to be, she needed his help, though she wasn't about to admit that to him right now, not with how his mind worked. An opening was the last thing she planned on giving him. It wasn't that she didn't find him physically attractive, but there was something about him that left her feeling cold.

* * *

'Mark's been after you ever since you and Craig where an item back in high school. I'm surprised you never noticed,' Lynn remarked once the waitress had taken their orders and left them alone at the small table. 'He's always had a problem with Craig.'

'Not always, they used to be friends,' she protested, giving her friend a sharp look. 'At least I thought they were.'

'No, not if you looked beneath the surface. Sure they hung out together, but there was that rivalry thing going on.' Lynn looked less than happy retelling the tale.

'That's just a teenage guy thing.' She took a sip from her glass of water.

'No, it's not, not in this case. He's had a crush on you for years, and when you started dating Craig the rivalry turned sour. It's been a thorn in his side ever since then. You've never let him get you in bed, have you?'

'Of course not,' she replied quickly, and couldn't fail to see the relief that washed over her friend's face at the news.

'And that's why he keeps coming on to you,' Lynn concluded cynically. 'He's not used to being turned down, and certainly not used to someone else getting the woman he wants. It's all competition, sure, but not the sort I'd wish my worst enemy to get caught up in. Ever noticed how alike they both are, long hair, arrogant, both well-built, but Craig's physique comes from the work he does and Mark spends hours at the gym trying to keep up his figure. And he didn't grow his hair long until Craig did. It's been a game of "whose the best" for years. You can bet if Craig hadn't been behind the plans for the lake that Mark would have found a way to get involved in them. I'm surprised you never noticed what was going on. It's not like you.'

'I'm blind as a bat if my heart is involved,' Anita admitted reluctantly. She'd really never thought about the similarities between the two men, not until Lynn pointed them out. How deep did they run? A part of her even wondered if Mark was as good a lover as Craig? 'Though looking back I can't believe I missed so many signs. I'll have to remember not to bring Craig up to Mark.'

'No kidding.' Lynn smiled. 'Well, you're not the first woman to be blind in love and you won't be the last. I think I've been that way more than once myself.'

'Who hasn't?' The more she found out, the more she felt like a fool who had been walking around with a blindfold on for the last ten years.

'So, are the rumors true, did you and Craig meet up last night?' Lynn nudged for the information as a friendly grin took the sting from her words.

'What?' The glass almost slipped from her hand. 'How

did you find out about that?'

'He asked you out in the middle of the street in front of three of the nosiest people in town. I'd be surprised if the most of the county didn't know about it by now. So, are you going to tell me, is it true, did you meet him?' She pressed, leaning closer across the table.

Anita could feel her face radiating heat as she shifted on the seat. 'Yes.'

'And?' Lynn pried.

'And what?' She didn't like where this was going and shifted her weight on the seat again, looking anywhere but at her friend. She loved Lynn like the sister she had never had, but there were times when she wished she would just drop things.

'What happened? Come on, you can't just leave it at "yes". You know I'm not going to stop asking you until I find out what happened between the two of you.'

'We met, we talked, I found out about the plans, and we parted ways as less than friends.' She couldn't meet Lynn's eyes.

'You fucked him, didn't you?'

'Lynn!' she hissed, glancing quickly around them to make sure no one else had heard. They were lucky this time; the diner was empty for the most part, only a handful of tables had one person sitting at them and they were at the other end of the room. If it had been lunch or dinnertime then within an hour most of the town would have been repeating the conversation.

'Well you did, don't deny it, I can see it in your eyes and

that blush speaks volumes, Anita. If you want to learn to hide things like that you need to learn not to blush.' Lynn grinned. 'So was he any good?'

'You are a terrible woman.' She looked around the restaurant in case the waitress was in hearing range. 'Yes, he was. Satisfied?'

'As long as you were.' Lynn smirked and leaned back in her chair.

The arrival of the waitress put a stop to the banter, but didn't do anything to ease the heat from Anita's cheeks, nor the flustered look she was sure could be seen from the other side of the room. She had been well and truly satisfied, that she couldn't deny. If he'd kept his mouth shut about the company she might have been satisfied more than once. There had been a moment in the lake when she had thought he was about to start the play all over again.

She tried focusing on her meal, but the silence, and the earlier comments by Lynn, had left her replaying the events of the night before. Her thighs pressed tightly together under the table, her skin tingling where he had touched her.

'Thinking about him again?' Lynn whispered conspiratorially.

'Well, he is worth the occasional thought,' she protested, focusing on her plate. 'But that's all he's going to be from now on, a thought, a fantasy on a quiet night, as there's no way I'm letting that bastard anywhere near me again.'

Lynn gave her an odd look. 'And just who are you trying to convince, Anita? Because it certainly isn't me.'

'Why do you say that?' She glanced up from her plate.

'Because you've had a crush on him for as long as I've known you and that didn't vanish just because he's involved in something you don't approve of. And who says that two people with different views can't put those views aside long enough to enjoy a little fun now and then?' Lynn spoke bluntly. 'I don't think my parents agreed on what time of day it was, but they were happily married for over thirty years and had three kids. I honestly think my pop would be a better man if mom was still alive to keep him focused.'

'Are you out of your mind?'

'Not in the least. Be honest with yourself, Anita, has anyone except Craig ever left you feeling at peace with yourself after sex?'

'When did you become my relationship councilor?' She wanted to sink under the table.

'It's part of being your friend. I'm just suggesting you think about it and don't close the door on enjoying yourself with him.'

'No, I'm not going to do this, Lynn. I'm not interested in anymore one-night-stands or brief relationships, especially with a man who I already know can't keep his mouth shut. He and some of his cronies were standing on the corner near the bank, laughing at me when I got out of the car. He's probably recounted the events on the beach to anyone who'll listen.'

'Oh, get over yourself, Anita. I seriously doubt Craig has done anything of the sort. He never said a word about you two the first time around, and he made damn sure anyone who spoke of it in his hearing got a piece of his mind. I know he left not long after that, but that rumor didn't come from him.' Lynn shook her head as she gave her friend a hard look. 'For an intelligent woman you can act like the town idiot at times. Use those research skills of yours and actually find out the truth instead of making assumptions.'

Chapter Six

Trying to get information from the DNR had been a nightmare, she had been transferred from one desk to another only to be told the person she needed to talk to wouldn't be back in the office until Monday morning. It had been her own fault, calling on a Saturday, but after the conversation with Lynn in the diner she'd been left flustered. The only real good that had come from the calls had been gaining the name and extension number of the person who might be able to help her. She still felt as though she were grasping at straws with information that might help, but it was a start. Not all of her research had been quite so frustrating, however, and she couldn't help but wish she had had the chance to talk with Mark before walking into the meeting, but she had barely stepped into the office before he grabbed her arm and his coat and pulled her towards the meeting hall. Any hopes she had held onto that she could discuss things in a quiet corner of the room vanished the minute she saw just how many people had already arrived.

'Just stick close to me. It looks bad in here and I'd prefer to keep you near me.' Mark kept a hold of her arm as they made their way into the room. Bodies packed the small town hall, leaving only the raised platform and table at the front of the room free for anyone to take a seat. Perhaps if she hadn't been attending the meeting with the owner of the local newspaper she might have had to suffer trying to hear everything from the press at the back of the narrow room, but several people noticed who she was with and made way for them both. After a few brief words she was even offered a chair, which she refused letting one of the older women take the seat instead as she moved closer to the front of the gathering.

Emotions already ran high and the meeting hadn't even begun. Raised voices and minor arguments kept breaking out between opposing mindsets, each one quickly brought to an end by those around them, with reminders that when the meeting began there would be time enough for all of that. It didn't do much good, though, because for each small argument that ended two new ones began.

'If they don't start the meeting soon it's going to turn in to an all-out brawl,' she muttered to Mark, who nodded in reply, his gaze firmly fixed on the table at the head of the room. Nothing else seemed to matter to him at the moment besides the arrival of the delegates. Maybe that was just his way with work, to get focused on what was going on so he could be professional.

They didn't have to wait much longer. As a shouting match gained life at the back of the hall the side door opened and five men walked in to take their places at the table. One of them was Johnson, the town Sheriff, a man she knew well possessed the longest fuse of any human being she had had the privilege of knowing. He would need that control today.

'Calm down all of you before I close the meeting and have you all sent to the school to do detention. If you're going to act like a bunch of rowdy school kids, then that's how I'll treat you!' Johnson addressed the room, his voice carrying easily all the way to the back.

More than a few people chuckled sheepishly at the threat, but it did the job and soon the room was both quiet and reasonably calm.

'That's better. Now, I know many here are all riled up about the plans, either being for them or dead set against them, but I want you to remember something here. This is a meeting, not a name-calling session. If you have concerns or questions, voice them, but if you want to turn this into a post-game brawl, the door is right there at the back. Kindly use it.'

The last of the laughter died away. Most people knew the Sheriff was serious and settled down, which allowed Anita to relax and finally look at the other remaining four men at the table. The Mayor, Mr. Dillerud, sat at the far left-hand side of the table looking older than his fifty years. In the last few months his hair had turned into a salt-and-pepper mix and the lines around his eyes had deepened. Next to him was the head of the planning commission, Mr. Baker, who shuffled through the papers nervously as he glanced around the room. Craig sat next to him. The man at the end of the table she didn't recognize, and she wondered if he was one of the men in Craig's employ.

'Since you've all settled down we can finally begin this meeting. The plans we're opening for discussion are the same that were laid out in the newspaper a few weeks ago, and there are copies pinned to the walls around the room if anyone needs to refresh themselves with the layout. Having said all of that I can now turn this meeting over to the four men involved in the main part of the planning. I'm just here to make sure you all behave.'

With a nervous cough Jake Dillerud pushed to his feet. 'I know the plans are not popular with everyone, but we need to think beyond sentiment here and-'

'Sit down, Jake. We all know you're for the plans, but we want to know how he's funding this building,' Mark called out as he pushed to his feet, holding a copy of his own newspaper in his hand. 'What about it, Craig, do you actually have the funds for all of this or is it going to crumble half way through and leave us with a ruin of a project at the side of what was once a beautiful lake?'

'I have the funds I need for the project, Mark. I wouldn't be proposing it if I didn't.' Craig pushed to his feet, his hands planted on the table as he looked over the room.

'And we just have to take your word for that?' Mark pushed.

'Yes.' Craig's gaze never left his old friend's.

'And is that what you told the people of Battle Lake?' Mark unfolded the Paper and pulled out a photocopied report.

'Battle Lake?' Anita whispered, glancing at the report, a question that more than a few others repeated.

'I see you've been doing a little digging, Mark,' Craig replied calmly. 'The incident at Battle Lake was a fuck-up, I'm the first to admit it, but that was not my doing. I had a backer and the papers were signed and approved when he was killed and his estate frozen over a tax issue. Unless you think I killed him off or tipped off the IRS about back taxes then you're barking up the wrong tree.' His arms folded across his chest. 'I also learned some very valuable lessons from that project. The money's already in place in my business account waiting to cover costs when we get the final go ahead.'

'*If* you get it.' Mark snapped. 'Just how is anyone here supposed to simply take your word for it about you having the money in place? For all we know that's what you told the people of Battle Lake as well.'

'Well I am sure if you'd done research on the situation you'd know just what had happened. What's the problem, Mark, didn't you bother to look any further into the details of Battle Lake or did you stop at the first hint of a problem you might be able to use?' Craig replied calmly above the growing noise.

'That is a situation I am still doing further investigation into.'

'I'd advise that you complete that research before you throw any more accusations my way, Mark.' Craig finally moved his gaze around the rest of the room. 'The plans are not going to please everyone, but I put a lot of research into the area, what facilities it was lacking, how the development would help those here, and yes, I know it's going to cause some disruption. The lake area will be changed beyond what most of you were expecting, but there will be no long-term damage to the lake or its inhabitants.'

'How could you possibly know if the work will cause long-term damage or not?' Anita pushed to her feet as she challenged him. 'Did you suddenly become qualified in environmental impact or gain the ability to see into the future?'

'No, I haven't become a psychic and I never claimed I had any environmental experience, but I have employed someone else who has skills in caring for the environment that I believe are needed for a project of this nature.' He waved his hand towards the unnamed man sitting at his side. 'David Kenson has spent the last ten years working with environmental agencies and has agreed to work with my company and he'll be watching our progress very closely.'

Her gaze moved from Craig to the mousy man next to him. 'I see, and will Mr. Kenson be willing to allow others to go over his credentials?'

'If that is necessary, then yes, I will,' David replied as he stood up. He couldn't have been much older than forty wearing a set of round, wire rimmed glasses that seemed to want to slip constantly from his nose. 'I have nothing to hide from you, or anyone else in this room. I'd be more than happy to provide copies of my work to anyone with an interest in the project, and I believe the information in those records will help to put a lot of concerns to rest.'

'I'm sure that is an offer many people here will be more than interested in taking Mr. Kenson up on,' she commented as she felt her arguments die, every thought she had to counter the plans with the impact to the environment, the birds she loved so much, even the peace and quiet, all faltering as she looked at the unimposing man.

'I'm sure they will, indeed.' Craig smiled as he cast his intense gaze around the room. 'Now, are there any other concerns?'

New voices were raised instantly asking how long it would take for the work to be completed and how the new businesses that would follow would detract from the ones already in place. Anita tried focusing on the comments, but her gaze returned time and again to Craig, at the intense look of concentration on his face, at the way he seemed to have an answer to everything. The air of confidence she had seen in him was well earned. The more she listened the more she came to understand that he was determined to build by the lake for what he thought were very good reasons, but that still didn't stop her from wanting to stop the work from taking place. No matter how the explanations were phrased, she just couldn't accept the lake being turned into a new community.

'And what about those people who already live near or on the lake? What about their wishes for the area?' Mark demanded. 'Are you just planning on pushing forwards without discussing it in person with those who'll have to wake up and see your new construction every morning for the rest of their lives?'

'I plan on taking part in some long and very intensive discussions with those most affected, one-on-one if I can arrange it.'

Was it her imagination or had Craig looked directly at her when he said that?

'Obviously they live out there for their own reasons, but I'm sure once they see the completed project they'll be happy with it. They may even enjoy becoming part of this new community.'

'What if we don't, Craig? Many of those who live there choose to do so for the peace and quiet, the lack of other people around.' She finally found her voice again. 'I've lived out there all my life. I don't move because I love the silence. I like being able to walk out onto my deck and see the birds swooping across the water at the end of the day. I do my best work out there, in fact. I'm seldom able to work anywhere else.'

'So you're accusing me of affectively ending your career?' he countered. 'Are you trying to tell everyone you're that poor a writer, Anita, that you can't work anywhere else?'

'I've tried working elsewhere and it's a lot harder. My trip to London only confirmed that.'

'So you want me to stop the work just so it doesn't interfere with *your* work? You want all this to stop just for you? That sounds more than a little selfish, wouldn't you say?'

'No, it's not just for me. If you'd been listening you'd know just how many people here don't want to see that building work take place. So some people here want it, but some don't. From just a quick headcount you've got a pretty even split going on here, and until the numbers are in your favor I don't believe the final approval can take place. Do you?' She drew on the small amount of information she had on the building regulations for the area. Maybe she was taking a risk as she hadn't had the chance to discuss the information with Mark yet, but it was the only weapon she had so far. 'You see, unless I'm very much mistaken, you want to build what would be a whole new township on land that was annexed by this town in nineteen-seventy-one.'

'I see you've done your research, Miss Burns. Very good to know, though I have to admit you've caught me a little off guard with this and it's something I'll need to look into.' The look he shot both Baker and Dillerud left her confused. Hadn't he known about the annexation?

'And when did the Mayor plan on informing the people about this?' Mark was back on his feet. 'Or was he trying to keep that from becoming common knowledge?'

'Are you accusing me of something?' Jake Dillerud demanded.

'Yes, I'm accusing you of having a personal interest in the development of the land at Lake Crane. Or would you rather admit to incompetence? And you, Rob, either you're incapable of doing your job or you've some incentive to keep the town from knowing they have the power to stop this right in their own hands.' Mark was in his element, or so it seemed. He finally had something concrete to attack the panel with. 'How many other people are in on this? How far does the corruption go?'

That was the final straw on the fragile hold that had kept the meeting from becoming little more than a brawl. Chairs tipped over, accusations rang out from every side of the room, men and women pushing forward trying to be heard. Anita stumbled as someone shoved her hard from behind. She reached out to try and steady herself as she cried out. Mark moved quickly, catching hold of her as he pushed through the crowd towards the wall, trying to find a safer place for them both.

Shouts for calm, for silence, rang out through the room, but no one seemed willing to listen until the booming voice of Sheriff Johnson sounded out, 'Enough! Clear the room! This meeting is over. Clear the room now, I say!'

She wasn't sure who opened the door at the back of the room or if it had always been open, but the press began to ease. Beneath the leadership of a voice they trusted, the men and women of the small town of Darvin headed slowly out into the street. The crush faded and she slowly came to realize she was sheltering in Mark's arms shaking like a leaf in the breeze.

'It's alright, we'll be able to move soon,' he murmured against her ear as he held her pressed against his chest. 'I won't let you be hurt, Anita. I never want to see any harm come to you, I never have.'

She had never heard him offer any form of care or protection to anyone before now; there had always been that brash 'Get them in bed' attitude. Yet now he cradled her tenderly.

'I'm fine,' she protested and tried to move out of his grasp.

'Like hell you are. I saw the look on your face. You're afraid.' He continued to hold her gently but inexorably. 'Just give yourself a few minutes to catch your breath.'

And lean against him. That's what he wanted as well, and he didn't have to say it in order for her to know it. There was something almost dangerous in remaining in his arms… a curiosity she had tried to suppress gained new life and for a moment she gave into it. Her eyes drifted closed as she leaned against his chest, listening to the sound of his heartbeat. The strength in his arms added to the feeling of comfort and safety. It didn't matter that she knew he was dangerous for her, or that he would most likely use her as a pawn to get to Craig, if that were possible. But the only way it would be possible was if Craig cared for her, and that opened up a new barrel of trouble she wasn't ready to look into just yet.

'Are you still up to your old tricks, Mark?' Craig's voice broke through her thoughts in the now near silence of the room. 'Taking advantage of a situation?'

The grip on her body eased a little, enough so she could step to Mark's side and still remain with one of his arms around her shoulders.

'He saved me from the crush of the crowd,' she explained. 'How you could see that as taking advantage of a situation?'

'Because I know Mark far better than you do, Anita. He doesn't do anything without a reason,' Craig explained as he walked closer. 'Though I'm sorry the crowd turned nasty, it wasn't something I was expecting.'

'Just like you weren't expecting someone to know about the annexation?' Mark probed, keeping his arm about her shoulder. 'And no, I don't have any plans with Anita, she's made things perfectly clear that we have a work relationship and nothing more. That is unless she decides otherwise. The decision is in her hands, not mine.'

There was the challenge. It might not have been spoken but she heard it nonetheless.

'Then if that's how things are you won't have any problem with me asking Anita to join me for a meal tomorrow night, will you?' Craig smiled as he spoke.

Mark's arm tensed about her shoulders, his voice measured as he answered, 'No, not at all, after all it's her choice, as I have already said.'

'Well, then, what do you say Anita? Will you join me for a meal tomorrow night? We have some unfinished conversations and a few matters I would like to clear up and apologize for. You have my word I won't try and change your mind about the building work at the lake.' His gaze turned to her, softening as it did so, hope written clearly in his eyes as he spoke.

Her first instinct was to tell him to go to hell and not bother to book a return ticket. She'd seen how the men with him had looked at her earlier in the day, but she could also hear Lynn's words from the restaurant. Craig wasn't the way she had allowed her anger to portray him, or so Lynn believed, and he did have the power to make her feel at peace with herself, to feel, if even only for a few moments, that she was loved. That word hadn't been exchanged between them, just two white roses figuratively left on her doorstep. 'Where would this meal take place?'

'How does the *Red Deer* sound? Seven o'clock tomorrow evening, and this time I won't be late, in fact, I'll be early,' he promised

Mark's fingers tightened on her shoulder. 'Are you sure about this, Anita?'

'Yes, I am, and yes, Craig, I'll be there, but if you are more than five minutes late I won't leave, I'll phone Mark and ask him to take your place at the table with me.' She spoke firmly. 'I won't be left waiting around for you or anyone else, and I'm very sure Mark would enjoy accompanying me for a meal.' That was a given, Mark would take it as the invitation he had been waiting for, she knew that, and was well aware of how hold cold her words sounded. She could only hope neither man realized that inside she was shaking, or that the wrong word from either of them would have had her retracting her declaration. She wasn't the bold, bright heroine she had created in so many stories, but for a moment she drew on the strength of those characters and met Craig's hard stare head on.

'I see, well, in that case, I'll make sure nothing comes up to delay me tomorrow night.' The warmth had seeped from his voice. 'I hadn't expected something like that from you,

Anita, but I don't blame you, either; I don't have the best of track records for arriving on time.' The words were begrudging but honest.

'Then I will see you tomorrow night.' She turned, stepping away from beneath Mark's arm to head for the door, but Craig was faster than she was and stepped in front of her.

'One more thing, Anita.' He stepped even closer, touching her face with his fingertips, trailing then down so he could cup her chin. 'I owe you far more of an apology than sending you a rose, more apologies than I will have the chance to offer in a lifetime, so I have no right to do this. I wouldn't blame you if you slapped me from here to the other end of the room, but I still have to try.' His fingers slipped back into her hair, tangling slowly within the silky red strands. He didn't move quickly, giving her every chance to pull away, but when she didn't him his grip tightened as he lowered his lips to brush against hers. She shivered, rising onto her toes as the feather-light touch deepened. Her lips parted willingly, giving in to the desire that came so willingly to life at his touch. It didn't matter that he was the enemy right now, that he threatened to destroy her life and her home. All she knew was the touch of his lips on hers, the feel of his tongue pushing into her mouth, stroking hers, teasing over the back of her teeth as he growled softly. She didn't know if the moan she heard was hers or one of her own imagination, but she clutched his arms, pressing deeper into the kiss as he nearly lifted her off her feet. Her nipples hardened beneath her shirt, a ripple of desire moving over her stomach as she felt the inner hand of her pussy tighten hungrily. Disappointment surfaced as he began moving back from the kiss, loosening his grip on her hair, his tongue slipping from her mouth as he nipped softly on her bottom lip.

'Thank you,' he whispered against her lips, the deep blue of his eyes holding hers.

* * *

'I can't believe you let him kiss you! What the hell where you thinking, Anita?' Mark demanded as the door closed behind them in the office. 'You know he's going to assume that dinner will lead to something more.'

'He can assume all he wants. And if it does lead to more that's between him and I, not you or anyone else.' Her lips still tingled from the kiss and she could taste the mint he had used to freshen up with before the meeting. How could one single simple kiss have left her feeling so alive?

'I'm trying to protect you, Anita. He'll do whatever he can to get this deal through and you know that.' Mark yanked open a drawer of his desk and pulled out a bottle of scotch. Papers lay scattered in a haphazard manner over his desk and for the first time she began to realize the staff he had possessed before she went to London was missing. She'd seen no sign of them since her return. Something had changed; Mark had changed in some way. 'You're walking right into his games, Anita.'

'Most people play games, men and women alike, it's human nature. But that kiss wasn't a game, and you'd be trying the same thing in his place.' She watched him pour a glass of scotch and lift it to his lips. Paint flaked from the walls in places, two of the light bulbs were out, and the jacket hanging from the hook near the door, the one he normally threw over his good clothes, had a rip in it. 'You'd do far more if given the chance and we both know it,' she added cruelly.

'Yes, I would, but not for the same reasons,' he retorted, swallowing the liquor. 'Yes I use people, I admit that, but I wouldn't do that to you. I've never wanted to do that to you.' She watched him as he poured a second drink before continuing. 'Yes a part of me always wanted you because he had you, there's always been a rivalry between us, games, women, liquor, cars, but that was only part of it. You're a beautiful woman and for the most part you've been a good friend, even when I've made some damn foolish mistakes.'

'What are you trying to do, Mark? Convince me that you're in love with me?'

'No... yes... I don't know. I'm just pissed you let him kiss you and you'll barely even give me a second glance. Things haven't been going my way in the last few months. Sales are down, advertisers are reluctant to take out space, and even more unwilling to pay the bills they have outstanding with me. Running things pretty much on my own, except for one man that comes in and helps me with typesetting before printing,' he admitted, downing a third shot.

'You should take it easy with those. Keep that up and you'll be drunk before the hour is up.' She reached for the bottle, trying to take it from him without success.

'I know what I'm doing, Anita. The question still remains, do you?' He argued.

'Yes, I believe I do.' So why did the words sound so hollow to her?

Chapter Seven

'You're enough to drive a man to drink,' Mark declared, pouring a new shot into the small glass. 'Can't you just cancel the dinner and, well… maybe join me for one instead?' He looked up as he put the bottle away at last.

'I thought you said it was my choice?' She took a step back from him, watching him closely. He'd given his word to behave but she could see he was ready to do something silly.

'It is. You don't see me trying to force you to change your mind, do you?' He put the glass down on his desk. 'Or perhaps you would prefer it if I did? Maybe I should march around this desk and grab your hair the way he did?'

'You're drunk,' she accused, though the idea of him kissing her the way Craig had was an intriguing one. After feeling the way he protected her from the crush in the meeting hall she was well aware he had a tender side to his nature he normally kept well hidden. Who did he keep that side of him for? There had to be a lucky woman out there for Mark.

'No, I'm not drunk, but I will be before the end of the night.' He grinned. 'Care to join me in getting nice and drunk? Maybe we can finally get to know each other.' He invited her closer with a sweep of his hand, knocking a file from the desk as he did so. Pictures scattered over the floor, sliding under chairs and desks. 'Shit!' He swore loudly as he scrambled to pick them up.

'Let me help,' she offered, beginning to collect the photographs. Most were shots taken around the local area, stock photography, no doubt, but one or two where of local people. No, of local women, the same women from what she could see. Though she didn't get a good look she could have sworn each of the women had brown hair caught back in a pony tail. Before she had the chance to see the woman's face clearly, Mark had snatched the photographs from her hands. His girlfriend, or just the woman he wanted to be with?

'Thanks,' he muttered, stuffing them back into the manila file and closing it before he put it out of sight in the desk. 'I get a little clumsy when I drink. Sorry. I don't always think things through, either, but I guess you kind of noticed that right now.'

'It would have been a little hard not to notice. Are you alright now?'

'I will be. I just need to sober up some. I don't suppose

you'd join me for a coffee?' he asked, though it was obvious he didn't expect her to accept the invitation.

'I have to get home, I need some sleep before tomorrow and I still have a few things I need to do. I tried the DNR today and I'll be trying again on Monday, but I also left a message that they might want to speak to you. One way or another we should get the information we need sometime on Monday. They might know a little more about that environmental advisor Craig has pulled in.'

'Good. I tried calling them today, but missed the man I needed to speak to. I didn't realize you'd also put a call into them already. As for David Kenson, he's not a local man, that's for sure. I'll see what I can dig up on him.' His eyes were already clearing with the idea of new work. 'We also need to look more deeply into the annexation and why the Mayor saw fit to keep silent about that.'

She nodded as he spoke. Jake Dillerud wasn't a bad man, so as far as she was concerned there was a good chance he simply hadn't known himself, but Rob Baker was another matter. He would have known, *should* have known. He was the one she needed to get more information about. He'd moved into Darvin about eight years ago, but apart from that she knew very little about him. 'Baker is the key; if we can find out what his interest in this, then we have something. I just can't believe Craig would deliberately keep the information from the town. Is there a chance he didn't know about it either?'

'Possibly, it depends on who was doing the research into the local planning and building regulations,' Mark replied, his brow furrowing. 'If he went by his father's old notes then there is a chance he did know, but a lot of those would be with Ray Gravy.'

'Lynn's father?' she asked, trying to keep the shock from her voice.

'He was Dawson senior's partner for eight or nine years. They parted ways after some contract fell through. I never knew the details.' He stood up and walked to a filing cabinet. 'There might be something in the archives. I'll need to start looking through the notes around here. My father kept extensive notes on all the local events and gossip. I still have most of them here and back at the house.' With the momentary self-pity thrown off, and the way he eagerly stepped back into his work, she could once again see the man that attracted so much attention from women. There was still that sense of ease and power about him even if things hadn't been going that well for him. And those problems she now began to understand had arisen from the threat of another newspaper, a new rival when the small town could barely provide enough customers to keep this periodical running at a decent level.

'It would seem there's a lot I wasn't really that familiar with,' she commented as she walked over to him. 'And I am sorry for any discomfort you felt when he kissed me. It wasn't meant as a jab at you in any way.'

'You love him.' He shrugged as he went through the paper work.

'I don't,' she protested, though the words sounded hollow even to her own ears.

'Don't try and lie to me about it. You've been in love with him since high school. That feeling didn't just fade into the background when he left or when you dated others. It doesn't stop me from feeling a little jealous about that, but I can't change how you feel. Maybe it's just time you accepted it as well.' He closed the cabinet and looked at her. 'If you can't, then in my opinion you should stop seeing him and come fuck *my* brains out.'

If he hadn't been smiling she would have become angry, but the smile and the glint in his eyes took the sting from his words. 'Well, that's something else I'll have to think about, isn't it?'

'Would it really be such a bad thing?' He took a step closer. 'I mean, if you let me kiss you the way you let him?'

'No, it wouldn't, but not tonight, you smell of cheap whisky and we both need to call it a day.' She didn't have the heart to say no, not when a part of her still wondered what it would be like to kiss him. 'I don't want to give you false hopes, Mark. I don't want to play games with your heart or your mind.'

'I'm not looking for a commitment, just a kiss, maybe a little more. Yes I'd love it if you felt towards me even a tenth of what you do for him.' His fingers brushed her cheek briefly before his hand dropped away.

'How could you possibly know what I feel for him, Mark?'

'Because I see it every time you look at him or mention his name. The light that appears in your eyes, the way the corners of your mouth twitch and form into a smile. That's not something you're very good at hiding.' He smiled himself as he spoke. 'There are only two women I've ever met who have made me feel the emotions I see in your eyes, and you're one of them.'

'Whose the other one?' she asked curiously.

'She's someone who I can't go near. I'd never put a woman in a position where she had to choose between her family and a man she might not even know exists.' He shook his head as he closed the subject. 'It might be best if we call it a night, I need to go get some sleep before those drinks make me say something I'll regret. Just remember, I need that report by the end of the week.'

* * *

Anita could barely focus as she drove back home; between Craig's kiss and Mark's declaration she was left feeling torn and unsettled. She wanted Craig, but Mark wanted her, and who knew what or who Craig wanted anymore? And who was the second woman Mark had mentioned, the one in the photographs she had only caught a glimpse of? She had felt familiar, but the quick look hadn't been long enough to identify her beyond the brown hair and pony tail. Just from that she could have been a good twenty different local women, and for all she knew he had met her elsewhere.

The distant lights of her small home beckoned. Even though it had been daylight when she left for town, she had two lights set on a timer ready to come on when it started getting dark. Even out in the countryside a dark house was an invitation for unwanted visitors. The last thing she had needed was to come home from London to find her house in turmoil. It was bad enough her heart was.

The narrow drive turned off away from the highway and wound past the tip of the lake. She stopped the car at the side of the old barn. Her family had never been proper farmers, but the barn was a holdover from the last family member who attempted to raise livestock some fifty years ago. 'Attempt' was the only way to put it from everything she had been told. The animals had either died or run away, except the one that had tried to kick her grandfather in the head. That had been the final straw. Since then not even a cat had been brought onto the land and the family had been a lot happier ever since.

'Love triangles… I thought they were a bitch to write about, but being in one is far worse,' she muttered as she filled a carafe with cold water and turned the coffee pot on. Even with the events in town she still had to get some work done on that manuscript, and she was in no mood to work any further on her research. How was she ever going to be able to think clearly enough to get the writing she needed done for the Paper? Perhaps if she let herself hide in worlds of fiction for a short time it would help.

The laptop booted up quickly and she settled herself down at the desk by the window. Even dark the lake offered a soothing presence that drew her in. Her fingers flew over the keys as she sank into the story and the world of ancient Celts, Romans and forbidden love. At least her stay in

England had helped with one idea and the words flowed over the screen…

The wind tugged at her raven hair, pulling it in long whipping strands across her face before it finally streamed behind her in a living banner. He loved the way her hair moved, the way the fires danced in her amber eyes. She was a thing of myth, possessed of a beauty the goddess Aphrodite herself would have envied, a creature he could not approach…

She scowled, hitting the delete keep as she wiped the passage from her screen. It was too melodramatic. Her editor would have sent a series of rapid emails to see if she was running a fever. With a sip of coffee she tried again…

He had never seen a woman like her, not from the seven hills of Rome to the shores of Gaul. She was fire, passion, beauty, all wrapped within the form of a woman who would have been better named a creature of Olympus. Fae child, that's what those foul Druid creatures might have named her. He wanted nothing more than to gather her into his arms and claim those sweet red lips, and yet there he stood at the front of his garrison sworn to wipe out her village to the last man, woman and child if they did not lay down their arms.

She growled, highlighting the passage before hitting delete again. What had gotten into her? She knew what she wanted to say, but every time she started it something else took over. There was no use trying to force it' the more she did the worse the writing would become, that much she was well aware of. With her coffee in one hand she closed down the file and opened up her e-mail instead. The manuscript could, and would, wait for a few extra days, long enough to get the last of whatever was bothering her out of her system. Or between her thighs…

The thought turned her face crimson with the rush of heat that swept across her skin. Maybe Mark had been half right – she wasn't in love with Craig, but she was deeply in lust with him. Love just didn't feel right to attach to his name, even though her heart skipped a beat when she gave the idea a brief moment of life.

Anita,
The date of the release party for Love's Sweet Turmoil has been moved up to the 1st of the month. I'm going to need you down in New York by the 30th, and you'll need to do a proof-read by the end of the week. I'm sending the file to you as soon as I hear back from you. Love Sue

That was all she needed! The book hadn't been set for release for two more months and now she barely had six weeks to get ready. With everything going on at home the last thing she needed was leaving on business again. But what choice did she have? The contract had been signed, and destroying the hard-won relationship with her agent and publishing house would likely end her career, or at least put her back on square one. If it wasn't one problem it was another.

Sue
Things are hectic here, but I'll be there. Send the copy. I'll look it over before the end of the week and send it back with any notes.
Anita

She typed up the reply quickly and hit the send button and stepped back from the computer before walking out onto the deck. The night sky was clear and the moon reflected onto the surface of the lake. She couldn't imagine what it would be like with the extra lights alongside the water. Would they be enough to make seeing the stars difficult or would she still be able to look up at the night sky and smile?

That was one of the small things Craig hadn't thought about or didn't care about. Could it be he had never noticed how bright the stars where by the lake and how dim they were when you looked for them in town? In a city they were almost impossible to see at all. She leaned on the railing and looked out across the water. Why couldn't love, or even lust, be easier than this? Strange how it worked out. In her stories there was always something that happened to allow the hero and heroine to finally patch the troubles between them, allowing them to end up together, maybe not married but certainly together. What would she have done if this had been nothing more than a manuscript she was working on, apart from throw it at the wall several times in frustration?

The coffee wasn't sitting too well in her stomach and she was more tired than she had allowed herself to admit. The only thing that made sense was to call it a night and try and get some decent sleep before she headed back into town the following morning. That was after she had breakfast with Lynn. Now *there* was someone she could rely on as an extra set of eyes to look over the proof copy. One thing she had learned was that it was very easy to ignore your own mistakes; a fresh set of eyes helped prevent a lot of problems. It was amazing the details Lynn could pick up on, just like when they had been kids and spotted that Indian arrowhead...

She nearly dropped the coffee mug.

That was the answer! Hadn't her Grandfather mentioned something about the lake being home to one of the local tribes several generations back? No, not home, but part of their hunting grounds? It was a long shot, but definitely worth looking into. If there were something of historical value around the area then that might buy them time or put a stop to the work altogether.

She hurried back to her computer and began to search through what few records she could find

It was nearly midnight by the time Anita collapsed across her bed, her mind filled with dates, tribal names, small battles, and violent storms that had raged across the county claiming lives and buildings in one swoop. The biggest lead she had come across dated from a storm that destroyed three houses at the edge of the lake in eighteen-eight-nine, but she wasn't sure what, if any, use the information would be. She needed to look at burial records. If there was a chance that some of the victims of the storm had been buried around the lake then... then she wasn't sure anymore. They couldn't force her to sell the land she lived on, but why would she want to stay and watch the area destroyed?

Sleep, a good night's rest would help, then she'd be able to look at the information with fresh eyes. Lynn would also be there come morning and could either read through the electronic proof copy or help with research. Between the laptop and her desk top computer she would be able to do both. At least that would keep her away from both men for a while. Great, what would Lynn say about the latest addition to the ongoing saga her life had become? That could wait until the morning. Tired, and with nothing else on her mind except the need to sleep, she slipped under the covers. She'd barely stopped since arriving back home and her body still hadn't caught up with the time difference. Her arm curled about the pillows as she turned onto her side, her eyes drifting closed.

Images of Craig mixed with those of Mark as endless pages of research drifted past her mind's eye. She turned in the sheets as they bound themselves more tightly around her body. Andrew's face turned into Craig's as she moaned under a kiss not knowing who it was that stole the breath from her body. She knew she was asleep, but that didn't seem to matter as the dream hands moved over her skin. She tried parting her thighs but the sheets wouldn't let her, so her mind turned the sheets into Craig's hands as he pinned her to the bed and teased her neck with butterfly-light touches of his lips. Even in sleep he made her feel alive, turned the inside of her thighs slick with the juices from her own needy pussy.

No, she wasn't going to give into the dream, not this time. She tried shaking herself free of the sheets and of the images, but they held fast. He held fast. His lips traced down over her breasts, nibbling, licking. She wanted to move so she could part her thighs and push up to meet him, but all he did was shake his head, teasing her further with the hard feel of his cock through the sheets. Why wouldn't he push the sheets away and thrust into her clenching walls? Because he wanted to tease her, to hear her beg, to make her tremble until she could take no more. Sex was about passion and control with him, somehow she had always known that, and it was one of the reasons she was drawn to him.

'Fuck me!' she pleaded. It didn't matter that he was a dream image, her body didn't care, it still reacted to his touch, real or imagined, still arched upwards towards him, pressed against the hardness of his cock that wasn't there. 'Please, fuck me...'

The sheets tangled further about her legs, his touch fading away leaving her trembling on the bed. Her hands clutched at the pillows as she moaned. There was nothing she could do, she was too weary to wake up fully and complete the arousal, and too turned on to simply shake it off. That didn't leave her a lot of options except to fall deeper into an unsettled sleep and the images that continued to plague her night...

* * *

She woke with a headache and eyes that felt as if she had been playing in the sand all night. Her stomach protested loudly as she pushed out of bed and headed for the shower. One thing the dreams (as annoying as they had been) had given her the chance to understand she was drawn to a certain type of man, to men who would take charge, and yet she also needed one that would understand her desire to write. Where was she going to find a man like that?

Her mind was far too ready to provide the answer in the form of Craig. He hadn't understood her interest in the lake, but he *had* been following her career. Perhaps he was more of a hope long-term than any man she had met before. Andrew had been a bastard, but for a short while he had filled the void, given her the strength and caring she had looked for in a man for long enough that she had been willing to overlook his mistakes. At least she had been until that moment in the car. What was it about her choice of men? She seemed to have a knack for picking the worst possible type for her, and what made it worse her body craved more. It didn't matter that the dream hadn't been real, she was still left with a tingling that played over the lips of her sex; a gentle throbbing in her clit that made each step towards the bathroom pure torture and a need to finish what the night had left incomplete.

Was there time to ease the intense longing the dreams had left her with?

A quick glance at the clock told her Lynn would be arriving within the hour and she needed to at least be awake enough to read through her e-mail. Lynn was an odd one, she rarely dated, seldom went out unless it was to run errands into town or drop by and speak with Anita, but a lot of that she blamed on Lynn's father. Mr. Gravy had to be one of the coldest men she had ever met. It didn't seem that strange to her that he had once worked with Craig's father; neither men were what she classed as easygoing. Even though she had seen Mr. Dawson spurn other people, mock them for letting friendships get in the way of money, he had always been fairly kind to her. She was caught between wanting to believe he was a good man and wanting to believe Craig. There were so many things slowly coming to light that she couldn't understand, not yet at least, but in time the pieces would fall into place, she hoped.

She had barely pulled her clothes on when Lynn arrived, as bright and cheerful as she always seemed to be. The shower had helped ease some of her other problems, and Lynn's arrival always made the day a little better. It didn't matter what was going on in the world, she always seemed to be full of life.

'Morning, sleepyhead. Got over the change in time zones yet?'

'Not yet, I still feel like I'm running on too little sleep, but I've been told it can take up to a week to shake off the jetlag completely.' Anita smiled and pushed a cup of coffee towards her friend. 'What about you?'

'So, so. Pop was in a mood this morning, but that's pretty much how he's been since Craig returned to town. He never did like your man.'

'He's not my man.'

'Not yet, but you want him to be. And from what I see he's more than willing to think about it or he wouldn't keep sending you roses every morning.' Lynn nodded to the third white rose she had brought in with her, this one still wrapped in yellow tissue paper. She handed it to Anita and relaxed into the overstuffed chair near the desk. 'I heard the meeting erupted into a brawl last night.'

'You weren't there?' she asked, surprised, as she added the new rose to the vase. If this kept up she'd need to find a second vase. The idea brought a smile to her lips as she walked over to boot up the two computers.

'No, it didn't interest me, but pop was there. He must have been as he came back with stories about you, Mark, Craig, a fight, and something about a kiss.' She grinned. 'So was it worth it, getting that kiss from him?'

'It was very worth it,' she admitted, the heat fading more easily from her cheeks this time. 'Though I didn't know someone else had seen it.'

'Several other people, from what I understand. Pop, Baker, Johnson and Kenson were all there. The way Baker is, you can bet the entire town knows by now, but then again its not something you are looking to hide is it?' she probed as she sipped her coffee. 'I wish I had a man like that in my life, one willing to kiss me anywhere he wanted, whenever he wanted. A man strong enough to… never mind.'

'No, please, go on, strong enough to what?' In all the years she had known Lynn, this was the first time she had heard her speak of love or of what type of man she wanted. 'I thought we talked to each other about everything?'

'We do, it's just that I haven't spoken about this to anyone.' She shifted in the chair, her long brown hair caught up in a pony tail at the nape of her neck curling over her shoulder like a wave of deep chocolate. 'I had the chance to do a lot of thinking when you were away. I spent more than a few nights here. I sat at your deck… I didn't think you'd mind me doing that.'

'No, why would I? I made it clear you can stay here anytime whether I'm here or not. It's the least I can do for the things you've helped me with over the years.'

'I got to thinking about why I didn't date, why I stayed away from men. It's not because I don't love someone, I do, or I think its love, but I look at my Pop and I see what men can become like. I'd rather spend the rest of my life without a man, even one I love, than see him turn into someone like my pop.' She didn't look at Anita as she spoke but rather let her gaze drift to the floor.

'Who is it you love, Lynn?' She set the mug down and walked over to sit on the edge of the chair.

'I'm not sure I'm ready to say his name yet…'

'I'm not about to laugh at you.' She rested her hand on Lynn's shoulder. 'You've never laughed at anything I've shared with you.'

'No you haven't, it's just… I'm in love with Mark!' she admitted, looking away from Anita as a blush spread across her cheeks.

'Mark? Our Mark?' The girl with the brown hair in a pony tail… had that been Lynn?

'Yes, Mark Taylor. I know, I know, I fall for the playboy of the town, the "fuck them and leave them" guy. God, what other choice do I have but to just stay home and try not to make a complete and utter fool of myself?'

'Or you could try and see if he shares the same feelings?'

She pulled Lynn close, her mind racing as she tried to figure out a way to help her friend. 'We make a right pair, don't we? You in love with Mark and me in love with the same man who wants to build around my lake.'

'And pop would call us both fools as he has no love for either man,' Lynn mumbled. 'You should hear what he calls them – bastards, bloodsuckers – and that's when he's in a good mood.'

'He's a piece of work your pop. Though I came across some interesting information yesterday. Did you know he'd worked with Craig's father?' She gave her friend's shoulder a quick squeeze before she got up from the chair.

'I heard something about that when I was younger, way younger, still in kindergarten, I think. I couldn't have been much older than that; he was trying to start his own business by the time I was seven, that much I remember from the paperwork he keeps around the house.' She pushed to her feet. 'I never did find out what had caused the split between them. The couple of times I tried talking to pop about it he shushed me up real quick.'

'He's is a strange man, we both know that,' she commented, trying to think of a way to cheer her friend up.

'You don't know the half of it. He takes up these strange hobbies. Like two months ago all he would do was sit and practice writing. At least I think that's what he was doing. He kept chasing me away anytime I came near. I'm not sure if he was practicing some form of calligraphy or what, all I saw were some signatures. Then a month prior to that he sorted through all his paperwork, years of the stuff, and that's why

I recalled him being in a partnership with Craig's father. Those were some of the papers I caught a glimpse of.'

This was something else she would have to look into when she got the time. There were so many small mysteries piling up in the back of her mind. Sooner or later she'd get the chance to look into all of them, Anita promised herself.

'There are some strange people in small towns,' she declared, and laughed as she pulled up her manuscript. 'We have some work to do. So, do you want to read through the proof copy or help with research?'

'Read or work, that's a tough choice.' Lynn grinned. 'I'll take read as my final answer.'

Chapter Eight

'I've been doing some digging and I'm not sure I like where this is going.' Anita sorted through the notes as Lynn handed her a new mug of coffee, tapping her pencil against the paper. 'Everything I'm finding points to Rob Baker knowing about the annexation ruling, and he would have had to have told Craig. So why it didn't become public knowledge I don't know.'

'That is unless Craig or someone else bribed Baker not to say something?' Lynn frowned as she sat down next to the desk. 'I don't like where this seems to be going as much anymore than you do. I don't like the idea of Craig being behind the bribes, but who else would have anything to gain from it?'

She stared at the paperwork and assorted notes scattered across the counter. 'Who else, indeed? I must be missing something here; there has to be another person who has something to gain from this.' The idea of Craig breaking the law, bribing officials and putting himself in a situation where he could end up spending years behind bars, made her feel physically ill. It just didn't make sense. He had always been more than a little headstrong and not above bending a few rules when he was younger, but this went so much further than she had thought him capable of.

'Mark might be able to find out more, and who has access to the information firsthand?' Lynn inquired, her brow furrowing as she tried to supply some ideas. 'There has to be something we are missing.'

'I think that would be Baker, the Mayor, and maybe a secretary or two. I'm not sure how many work in that department, it's not as though we have a huge city here, so the information would only pass through a few hands at most.' She pulled out the handwritten notes and scanned through them before finally putting them away in her desk. 'I need a break. When the words start blurring one into the other then I've done too much.' She tried laughing about the situation as she spoke. 'This is why I prefer writing fiction, I still have to do research, but not as much. Writing articles all the time would drive me nuts.'

'I thought being insane was a requirement for writing?' Lynn joked as she shut down the laptop. 'I've left a document in your files with the couple of problems I spotted in the proof copy. Just minor things, a few typo's and spacing issues.'

'Have you ever thought of becoming an editor, professionally, I mean? There's a need for good independent editors these days with the amount of self-published works out there.'

Lynn shrugged. 'I wouldn't know where to start trying to look for work.'

'I can ask around when I go to the launch,' she offered. Lynn would make a good editor, with a little guidance. She always seemed to be able to spot holes in plotlines and offer possible solutions, and she didn't try and change the voice of the story. 'It's just a thought, if you're interested. I've got a few books on the subject somewhere in the library.' She nodded towards the large room at the back of the house. Over the years she had collected over a thousand research books, on top of her own reading material.

'Sure, it's worth a try. I might as well do something I enjoy.' Lynn was one of the lucky ones. Through luck more than anything else she didn't have to work in order to keep a roof over her head. She still lived with her father, though that was part of the situation Anita didn't envy, and thanks to her mother Lynn had been left with a small yearly allowance from an inheritance. A carefully drawn out Will had made sure it was money her father could never get his hands on. 'Aren't you supposed to be meeting Craig for dinner at seven?'

'Yes, but I've got plenty of time, it's only…' She turned to glance at the clock. 'Five thirty! Shit, I didn't realize how long we'd been working. I still have to shower and get ready.' She turned and nearly ran for her bedroom. 'I've no idea what I want to wear, either. *The Red Deer* isn't exactly a jeans and sweater place.'

'Is that where he's taking you? Nice. I didn't think he'd be taking you there again, not with the disaster his birthday party turned into.' Lynn followed her into the bedroom and started hunting through the closet. 'What about the black dress you wore for that signing?'

'That might work,' she agreed as Lynn pulled the dress out. 'Yes, that will work just fine. The matching shoes should be in the bottom of the closet and I need to do something with this hair.'

'I wish I had your coloring, red hair and a black dress. Simple but stunning, you'll knock him dead.' Lynn grinned and pulled the shoes out.

'I have no desire to knock him dead. Knock him on his back and ride him hard would be far more interesting.' She was only half joking.

'Then I suggest real stockings, not the hold up kinds. The minute he realizes you're wearing a garter belt he'll be drooling and not just from his lips.'

* * *

The Red Deer was a place Anita hadn't stepped foot into in over five years. The restaurant had been a part of the town for as long as she could remember, passing down through one generation to the next, and the food had only improved as the years went by, if the rumors where to be believed. Now, at least, she had the chance to look around as she waited for Craig. She had arrived early, and had hopes he would be on time just as he had promised because she had every intention of calling Mark to take his place if he was a single minute late.

'Would you like something to drink while you're waiting?' A blond-haired waitress inquired as Anita sat down in the small lounge.

'Just a glass of water for now. I believe there's a table for two booked in the name of Dawson?' It wouldn't have surprised her to learn that Craig had forgotten to book the table, so it came as a pleasant relief when the black-and-white clad waitress confirmed the booking and moved away to fetch the glass of water. That was one worry lifted from her mind, and it confirmed that he was at least planning on arriving for the meal. It didn't matter who she was dating, she always had this near irrational fear of being stood up. It had never happened to her, but that hadn't done anything to ease the fear.

She kept glancing towards the door as she sipped her water. Mark would be all too willing to take his place if Craig didn't show up, though that would open up a new set of problems, more than she had even counted on originally now that she knew about Lynn's feelings for Mark. She had to find a way to help her friend. Mark needed a good woman in his life and Lynn was certainly that. She was one of the few women Anita knew who would put everything on hold for someone she cared for. If Lynn ever realized just how many of the heroines she wrote about where based on her she'd turn a permanent shade of red. Lynn had spent over an hour helping to get her ready; helping her search for a good pair of stockings after which they struggled to get her unruly hair into something other than a braid. By the time the two women had finished Anita felt very presentable, indeed.

'Hello, Anita.' Craig's voice roused her from her thoughts. 'As you see, I can be on time when I want to be.'

Her gaze moved upwards, lingering on his chest before meet his. She'd never seen him in anything other than jeans and a t-shirt before. This evening he wore a pair of dress slacks, a pressed shirt and a tie. She hadn't even known he owned a tie before tonight. The sound of his voice had other, mainly hidden, effects on her. Her body desired his touch, wanted to feel his fingers against her skin and his cock buried in her cunt. Her nipples hardened under the dress. It took every ounce of self control she possessed to focus on his eyes as she spoke and not think of his lips touching her neck, or claiming a ripe nipple… 'So it would seem, Craig.'

'Is that all I get?'

'Just what where you expecting from me, a standing ovation?' she replied, her smile matching his.

'A "nice to see you" would have worked just as well.' He offered her his arm.

'Well, it *is* nice to see you. I have to admit you do clean up quite well.' She took his arm.

'And you, I think the last time I saw you in a dress was the high school Prom.'

Heat crept across her cheeks. 'Well my taste in dresses has changed since then.'

He brushed his fingers across her cheek, letting them trail down her neck to linger on a shoulder left bare except for a thin strap. She shivered beneath his touch, nearly biting her lip to keep a low whimper from escaping her. What did she become when she was near him? He only had to touch her and she wanted more.

'And you'll hear no complaints from me on that change. It's not that I didn't like that dress for the Prom, but it did... well, cover you.'

'I believe that was the idea when mom helped me pick it out.' That had been the last outfit her mom had been around to choose for her, less than a year later she was dead. Her dad had passed away several years before and in some ways her death had helped settle things for Anita after Craig's disappearance. She had been able to make some strides in her career, though the first three manuscripts had been rejected as too bitter-sweet. The market had only been interested in happily-ever-after-endings back then, now things where changing, albeit slowly.

'She was a good woman.' Craig held her close against him. 'I'm sorry I never came back for the funeral, I should have, but there are a lot of things I should have done. I just hope I get the time to apologize for them all.'

She could hear the regret in his voice. 'We all do things we later feel we shouldn't have done and I include myself in that, Craig.'

He nodded, whispering into her hair, 'Well, shall we see if they have that table ready for us, or did you just want to stand here in my arms all night?'

'That wouldn't be such a bad way to spend the night, though the meal would be a better choice, at least this time,' she replied shyly. She could have stayed within his arms for hours listening to his heart beat, feeling his voice reverberate through his chest into her body. Even beyond the desire he could release in her, she felt safe in his arms.

'If you insist,' he teased and escorted her into the body of the restaurant. Low lighting added to the warm feeling in the main room. Small tables were set at comfortable distances from each other, each one adorned with its own small candle. A stand of wrought iron stood next to the table they approached holding an ice bucket and a bottle of wine. 'I hope you don't mind but I called ahead and had them prepare a few things,' he told her.

'Why would I mind?'

'I'm not sure, but this isn't something I make a habit of doing.' He pulled out a chair for her to sit. 'Normally a meal for me is the nearest diner or a burger on the way back to the motel.'

She glanced at him when he took the seat opposite hers, trying hard not to let her mind explore what he looked like without his shirt on. 'I suppose a lot of the time you end up living from one motel to the next,' she mused.

'For the most part, yes, though I've slept in some strange places in the last few years. More than a few motels I wouldn't want to send my worst enemy to. Then there have been those rare times I've been invited to stay at another crew member's house. For a short while it's almost like becoming part of the family, especially if he or she has kids. I'm an honorary uncle to more kids than I can keep track of these days.'

'There are a lot of women working construction then?'

she asked, it was something she had never really given a lot of thought to. Construction sites, to her, brought images of loud men with a large amount of ass cleavage showing, hanging over railings on sites as they hassled passing women with catcalls, wolf whistles and embarrassing comments.

'Not that many, but the bigger the site the more women seem willing to try out for work. Some of the best welders I know are women.' He smiled as he poured the wine. 'They have a good eye for detail, though most of the men I work with would disagree. There's still a feeling with some teams that women shouldn't be there, but that attitude is changing slowly.'

'It takes time.' His line of work was something she knew very little about beyond the research she had recently found herself doing. 'So how did you get the money to start your own business? It couldn't have been easy.'

'I worked every day I could, lived as basically as I could, and went from there. It's not cheap, and it can be more than a small risk every time I put a bid in. You can do the work, pay out for materials, and then not always get paid on time. Sometimes you don't get paid at all, but you've still had to pay for the materials and the wages. I'd say over fifty percent of companies go bust in their first year.'

'I never thought about it that way,' she admitted.

'Most people don't. It's not something I knew about until I started looking into the business end of things and not just working on sites.'

She looked over the menu, trying to focus on the listings instead of listening to the voice at the back of her mind that screamed the risk would explain why he had bribed Rob Baker into keeping his mouth shut. 'I'm guessing that a few companies take steps to make sure contracts go through and work gets completed?' she tried to sound casual.

'A few do, yes, but that's not how I operate,' he answered in a calm voice. 'That is what you were implying, wasn't it?'

She shifted in her chair and set down the menu. 'Was I that obvious?'

'To be blunt about it, yes, you were.' But he didn't appear to be that upset. 'I get asked that sort of question every couple of weeks, so I am used to it. Too many people have been watching cop shows and bad movies.'

'So would you mind if I contacted you when all this business with the lake project is over if I need some background information for a storyline?' she asked, watching his face for a reaction.

'I'd love to help out, if I can.'

The conversation died for a short while as the waitress returned to take their orders and that gave her the chance to look at him closely again. Each time she had seen him since his return to Darvin she had noticed something different. Now she had the chance to see how he acted in a setting she would never have pictured him in. He spoke in a clear but soft voice, enunciating the words carefully so the waitress could not mistake what was being ordered. The shirt wasn't brand new, so he'd had call to wear it before. Perhaps he'd used it for business deals, dining potential clients? Her breath caught in her throat as he looked at her. She couldn't help the fact that her body responded every time she saw him.

'So why isn't there a Mrs. Dawson?' It was a question she had wanted to ask the minute she realized his ring finger was bare. She'd always imagined he had found himself a woman willing to do whatever he wanted in life, had settled down and was helping to raise a dozen small children. Well, not quite a dozen, but the idea was the same. When she'd noticed the lack of a ring, or any other signs that he was married, the relief had been strange. How would she have reacted if her fears had been realized?

'I never came across another woman I wanted to spend the rest of my life with.' He looked directly at her. 'I'm not going to hide the fact I wanted to marry you and walking away from you was the worst mistake of my life.'

'You don't have to say that, Craig,' she protested, but this time she couldn't stop the heat from radiating across her face.

'Why not, it's the truth.' He reached across the table and caught hold of her hand. 'You're the only woman I've ever loved, Anita.'

She wanted to deny it, to lower her gaze, to break away from the intense look in his eyes. She'd waited so long to hear those words from him and now they sounded almost like a death knell in her heart. If she was right and he was responsible for bribing Rob Baker, then he'd spend more than a few years in jail. How would she handle that, being in love with a man who was behind bars? No, she wasn't ready to think about that, not just yet.

'What about you, has there been a steady man?' He didn't say the word 'husband' which struck her as odd, until she remembered he had been following her career. 'Or have you been too busy?'

'I've dated on and off.' She broke away from his gaze at last, though it wasn't easy. 'The last man nearly put me off dating for life. He expected me to give up my writing for him, just pack everything up, leave my home and move to England to be with him.'

'Sounds like a jerk, in fact, he sounds a lot like I used to be,' he joked, trying to lighten her mood. 'Perhaps he'll grow out of it in time?'

'Well if he does I won't be around to see it. And you were nothing like him. You asked me to leave my home, but you never asked me to stop dreaming.'

'I came close to it, though,' he admitted, squeezing her hand gently. 'I wouldn't do that now, though. I've seen the work you've done. It's not my first choice of reading material but I have learned to enjoy it. You're a good writer, Anita, and I've even taken one or two of your books to work.'

'You did?' She tried to imagine him reading a romance novel on his lunch break in the midst of a group of men looking through newspapers or copies of *Penthouse*. 'I bet you got a few interesting comments about that.' She smiled.

'A few, but it was worth it. I even got a couple of others buying your books once they had taken a look at the style of stories you write. Of course they all claimed it was for their mothers or girlfriends.' He laughed, brushing his thumb slowly and gently against her palm. 'I'm sure those women did get to read the books eventually.' He broke contact with her as the food arrived, but that didn't stop the tingling from traveling along her arm. She could still feel his touch even when she reached for her fork and began to eat.

* * *

'I hadn't expected you to be there this evening,' he whispered into her hair as they walked through the small town park. Dinner had been wonderful. In the short time they had talked through many of the small misunderstandings they had had, then the topics had ranged from her work to his and everything in between, carefully avoiding any mention of the lake. 'I really thought I would arrive and find you had left or were sitting down for a meal with Mark. I'm not sure what happened to ruin the friendship he and I used to have. There was a time we would have gone to the line for each other, but now I doubt he would spit on me if I was on fire. I know some of it dates from you and I getting together, but there's got to be more to it than that. He blew up suddenly, about a week before the Prom and I never found out why.'

'People change, but I hope one day you and he can figure things out.' She leaned closer to him. They had agree to walk off some of the meal together, though she knew she couldn't walk too far in the heels she had chosen to wear. Few people walked through the park at night apart from the occasional couple in search of a little privacy, or high school kids trying to get into mischief.

'Maybe, but I'm not going to hold my breath on that. Besides, I'm well aware that as long as I show any interest in you, and you return that interest instead of returning his interest, there'll be a problem.' He stopped and turned her to face him, his hands holding her arms gently. 'Are you interested in him at all? If you are, all you have to do is say the word and I'll back off. I don't want to cause you any more trouble than I already have.'

She did feel something for Mark, but not what Mark hoped for, and certainly not something that would require Craig stepping back. 'No, I don't. He's good looking, but I've never taken any steps with him, it just wouldn't work.' She wouldn't mention Lynn; it wouldn't be right to share her confidence with him.

'Good, that means I don't have to hold back something I've been wanting to do all night.' He pulled her into his arms, one hand tangling into her hair as he brought his lips down to cover hers. His free hand traced down her back, cupping her ass as she parted her lips beneath his willingly. She moaned at the invasion of his tongue, trembling softly in his grasp as his tongue explored her mouth without hesitation or mercy. Her body pressed against his, her stomach digging into the buckle of his belt, her carefully arranged hair turned into a passionate mess under the tightening of his fingers. She all but forgot how to breathe as her tongue danced with his. Slowly he pushed them both back across the path and into the grass, only his grip on her body preventing her from stumbling, his lips never leaving hers until she felt a tree against her back. 'I want you, Anita. I've never stopped wanting you,' he groaned.

'What if someone sees us?' she protested, though her heart wasn't in the words. 'We'll be caught…'

'No, we won't, trust me,' he reassured her, nibbling soft

kisses along her shoulder, the grip on her hair vanishing as he pulled at the hem of her dress. 'I won't let anyone see us. I want to taste you, to know every part of you.' He raised her dress to her waist and tugged her panties down to her ankles in one swift move. 'A garter belt… damn, woman, if I had known you were wearing these we'd have skipped dinner.' He dropped to his knees and breathed across the soft curls that covered her mound.

Her fingers dug into the tree behind her, her thighs parting at the light touch of his tongue. 'You can't mean to… oh!' Her hips jerked, pressing forward against his face as his tongue delved between the lips of her heated sex. He trailed the tip of his tongue across her clit before closing his lips on the throbbing nub. She reached up, grabbing hold of a low branch above her head, trying to balance herself as he suckled hungrily on her clit. She couldn't do this, they'd be caught, someone would see them and she'd have to live with that for the rest of her life while he moved on with his work just as he'd done all those years ago. 'God!' A finger pressed deeply into the pulsing walls of her pussy, working slowly in and out as he trapped her clit between his lips, circling it with his tongue rapidly. Protests formed and died on her lips with each slow thrust of his finger, and then vanished completely when a second finger slid in to join the first. Her cunt tightened, trying to milk the invaders, her hips rocking forward, pressing close to his face, moving with a wanton life of their own. Her body didn't care if anyone found them, it didn't care if half the town suddenly turned up to cheer them one, it only knew the delights he was inflicting on her.

A soft breeze played through the park, adding its own light touch to her aching breasts and taut nipples. Fear added to the desire he created at the idea of being caught with his lips on her clit and his fingers buried deep in her pussy. Would someone stop them before he could finish or would they watch and find themselves aroused in return?

'Fuck my fingers!' he growled as he pushed them deep into her body. 'Fuck back against them for me.' His voice reverberated through her pelvis as her hips pushed forward, rocking down onto his hand as a soft cry escaped her. Her hands tightened on the branch above her as she used it for leverage, rising upwards before plunging back down onto his hard fingers, crying out as they hit that hidden spot deep in her cunt. 'That's it, I want to hear you come from fucking my fingers. I want to suck your clit as you fight not to scream.' His words inspired her to move harder and faster onto his stiff digits, the touch of his tongue on her clit, the way his lips rolled the throbbing nub between them, the near painful pleasure each time his fingers touched her G spot, all wildly encouraged her. Pleasure built into a need so powerful she couldn't have stopped her hips from rocking if the entire United States Marine Corp had suddenly appeared.

She wanted to cum, needed to cum, but still her hips rocked. Her thighs shook, a quiver ran across her belly, her arms ached from the force with which she held onto the branch, and still she fucked down onto his probing fingers. Desire flooded from her pussy, soaking his hand, her clit throbbing until she swore it would explode with the sensations he inflicted on her with wicked and fast flicks of his tongue. Then she could fight the need no longer. Her thighs locked, her hips pressed forward fully against his face, her hands lost their grip on the tree to find a new one in his hair, clenching tight. She tried not to scream and clamped her lips tighter than ever before, but still a low, strangled cry rang through the park in the moments before her knees finally gave out.

Her body trembled as he pulled his fingers from within her tight walls, her body almost unwilling to release them. With a soft whimper she let him ease her to the ground, barely noticing that her panties lay beside her.

'Now that was well worth waiting for,' he murmured against her neck, pulling her to nestle half in his lap as he sat against the tree. 'You taste just as sweet as I remembered.'

'I can't believe I let you do that,' she gasped, pushing a strand of hair back from her face.

'Well you did, and I do believe you enjoyed it a great deal, either that or you moonlight as an actress and forgot to tell me.' He held her close on his lap. 'Though we can't stay here much longer, someone might come along to investigate and I wouldn't want them interrupting round two.'

'Round two?'

'That's if you would like to continue this elsewhere, somewhere with a bed perhaps?' he suggested, catching her earlobe between his teeth and nipping lightly.

'Take me home, Craig, please. Take me home and make love to me in my own bed,' she pleaded, shivering at the thought of what would happen if he agreed.

'As my lady wishes,' he replied with a laugh, slipping her from his arms only long enough to stand up before sweeping her back into his grasp and nestling her head against his chest. With long and easy strides he walked back out of the park towards his waiting truck. It was only when they were half way to her house that she finally remembered her panties were lying on the grass next to the tree.

Chapter Nine

The door closed behind them as he carried her into her bedroom. She could have teased him for carrying her, joked about him acting chivalrous as if he was taking a part from a story, but she was enjoying the feeling of being in his arms far too much. There was something almost innocent about it, although having the memory of his wicked tongue so fresh in her mind she was only too well aware neither one of them was innocent. Neither one of them could have claimed to be innocent after the way they had both behaved in the park. Never again would she be able to look at the trees there in the same way. What would people think when they found her panties? At least she was long past the age where she needed to have her name on them. The drive home had been just as interesting. He had a wicked tongue in more ways than one and had taken great delight in describing all the things he wanted to do to her once they reached her house.

'I've never been in your room before,' he commented as he lay her gently down on her bed.

'Well you can't say that after tonight.' She smiled up at him, reaching up to touch the side of his face, her fingers playing with the strands of long, dark hair that hung forward over his eyes.

'No, I can't.' He sat down on the edge of her bed, looking down at her as he caught her hand, bringing it to his lap. 'You didn't tell me to stop, back in the park. You protested, but never told me to stop, yet I knew you were afraid at first.'

'Would you have stopped if I had asked?' The small voice of doubt gained a moment's life and voiced the question she had hoped to keep silent.

'Of course, as much as I wanted to do that, I wouldn't have forced it on you, I'm not like that. There's a big difference between taking charge and forcing someone, Anita. I'd never force you or anyone else to do something they truly didn't want to do. All you ever have to say to me is "no".'

The doubt protested, tried crying out that he was lying, but she could see the emotions playing across his face – the moment's hurt that she had asked, but an understanding that she had needed to know for her own peace of mind. If he had been truly angry, or if she had seen anything that offered a hint of the danger she had seen in Andrew, then it would have been over, between them, she knew that now.

Somehow she'd have come up with an excuse for him to leave and she would have made very sure he never came anywhere near her again. 'I had to ask,' she explained.

'I understand, I probably would have asked myself if the situation had ever occurred with me.' He frowned a little, almost wincing. 'All right, that sounds odd, I can't ever see myself in a situation where a man is pinning me to a tree and going down on me. Now, if *you* were to try, I might actually let you.'

'Ah, is that an invitation?' She smiled.

'Why bother to find a tree when we have a bed right here?' He replied, matching her smile. 'Unless, of course, it's not something you'd like to do, but only something you enjoy teasing about.'

Using her mouth on a man wasn't her favorite activity, for the most part it scared her, but with Craig she was willing to try it. 'No, but I don't have a lot of practice with this, so if I do something wrong...'

'Anything you want to do will be just fine with me.' He brushed his fingers across her breasts, avoiding her nipple. 'If you don't want to do it, just say so, I don't mind.'

She rolled onto her side and slipped down from the bed, moving to her knees at his feet. She wanted to do this, needed to try and push past her discomfort at taking a man into her mouth. She loved the feel of what he had done to her and knew she could give him at least some of the pleasure she had felt. Nervously, she reached for his belt as he parted his thighs, allowing her to scoot closer to him. Her hair fell over her face, blocking some of the blush she could feel on her cheeks. The belt opened, his pants following a moment later, allowing her to see more clearly the growing bulge of his cock. He wanted this, most men did, but he at least was willing to let her take her time.

'Remember, you can stop any time you want to, Anita. I won't grab you, if that's what you're afraid of,' he reassured her, and placed his hands on the side of the bed, gripping the edge.

That helped, she knew a lot of men liked to grab the back of a woman's head when they used her mouth. In time she might enjoy that, even welcome it, but for now she needed to both know and feel that she was in control. 'Thank you,' she replied, looking up at him through her hair for a moment. Taking a slow breath, she lowered her gaze back to the swelling outline of his cock, still hidden under the white cotton of his briefs. Gently, she reached into his pants, easing him free of the cotton until his erect penis throbbed in her grasp. Fear took hold of her as she wondered how she could fit all of him in her mouth. Maybe she didn't have to, not yet at least.

Her fingers circled his base, closing firmly as she lowered her head to his glistening tip and placed a soft kiss to the delicate skin. His erection throbbed in her hand at the touch and a low moan of pleasure escaped him. She smiled, the sound encouraging her to continue as she trailed soft, light kisses over the head of his cock, licking slowly over the tight surface before closing her lips on the tip for a brief moment and suckling hard. He groaned loudly, his penis jerking as she pulled back from him, and she half expected him to grab for her head, but the move never came as he continued grasping the edge of the bed.

Smiling, she licked slowly down the underside of his cock, squeezing and releasing about the base, taking her time to reach what her fingers had him firmly trapped. Each touch, each squeeze, brought another tight jerk from his trapped flesh, ones now matched by a deep clenching in the walls of her sex. It was as if she could still feel his fingers buried deep inside her, pushing up each time he twitched in her grasp. Her tongue curled about him as she caught the underside of his erection in her lips, suckling just under the head and working her mouth down towards her fingers. His groans intensified, but still he didn't grab for her head.

With a wicked delight she captured the head of his cock between her lips, running her tongue over it, circling it as she suckled softly. She could taste him now, a mixture of sweet and salt combined, a flavor that didn't send her running for the hills the way she had feared. As her confidence grew she took more of him into her mouth, pressing her tongue against the underside of his erection, suckling, licking, humming on his flesh as it began to fill her mouth. Her free hand moved, reaching into his pants to cup his balls, one finger rubbing gently behind his sack as she massaged the warm flesh in her palm. The taste became stronger as she pressed lightly, encouraging her to rub a little faster there, to suckle just a little harder as she took as much of him into her mouth as she could. The fear of gagging hit her, and for a moment she stopped, shaking, pulling her mouth from his cock as she pushed the emotions back.

'You don't have to continue… oh!'

Her lips claimed his cock again, suckling as she pushed down to meet her fingers, pressing him to the roof of her mouth, circling her tongue around him, wrapping him tight, unwrapping, all in time to the slow squeezing of her hand.

'God, Anita! Where did you learn to do that?' he groaned, his cock throbbing heavily in her mouth. 'I can't... I know I can't hold on much longer, not like this.' His hands grasped her shoulders, pushing her away gently. 'I want to come inside you, but I won't, not in your mouth, not if you're not ready.'

She nodded, pushing back to her feet. As much as she wanted to be able to say 'yes' the idea frightened her too much right now; she wasn't ready to do that just yet. Her dress fell from her body, her bra following quickly before she crawled onto the bed. 'Fuck me, please. I want to feel you come inside me.' She rolled onto her back as he shed his clothes, waiting naked on the bed for him except for her stockings and garter belt.

'You're a wicked woman still in your stockings.' He traced a light touch over the belt. 'Beautiful, sensual, and wicked all rolled into one. I count myself as a lucky man.' He lay next to her for a moment, and then he moved, rolling on top of her, his lips claiming hers in a kiss that left her gasping. Her thighs parted with an eagerness she hadn't known existed, her cunt clenching with the need to feel his cock buried inside it. 'I'm not going to fuck you, Anita.'

Her heart sank.

'No, I'm not going to fuck you, my love. I'm going to make slow and delicious love to you.'

* * *

Long fingers of daylight reached through the window, leaving a pattern of warmth across her naked body. The sheets had long since been kicked to the floor. He had teased her, tormented her with soft kisses and light touches until she had begged to feel him in her cunt. The last thing she could remember was coming hard, screaming his name. She had slept without dreams for the first time she could remember, and now woke rested in his arms. His cock nestled against her thigh, still semi hard, and her body well remembered the pleasure he had been able to bring to her.

Almost regretfully she moved from the bed, slipping from his grasp as he rolled over and grabbed the pillow she had used, hugging it to his body in a sleepy satisfaction. Perhaps he was awake enough to know she had moved, but she wasn't about to test that by speaking to him. Without a care for him seeing her naked in the full light of day, she walked into her bathroom and turned on the shower.

With the water massaging her body she let her mind drift over the time she had spent with Craig. She hadn't meant for the night to end with them in bed, she hadn't thought beyond the meal and spending some time with him, but it had happened and in all honesty she didn't regret it. He was a good man, wasn't he?

'Anita?'

She heard him call out as she stepped out from the shower and wrapped a towel around her body.

'I'm here,' she replied and walked back out into the bedroom, a second towel wrapped around her hair. 'I was just taking a shower. I hope I didn't wake you up?'

'No, I was waking up anyway.' He rolled out of bed. 'Mind if I take a shower myself?' 'Help yourself.' It would give her chance to catch up on her e-mails, or at least get dressed. By now there might have been a reply from some of the sites she had contacted for aid, though she felt a little strange trying to check for information while he was there.

'Thanks.' He smiled and walked past her into the bathroom. She turned to watch him and for the first time noticed a long scar on his back. A white and jagged line marked a path down from his left shoulder blade to the small of his back. She wanted to stop him and ask where it had come from, but he needed the shower and there would be time enough to find out over breakfast.

With the sound of the water running, a clean pair of jeans hugging her thighs under a baggy t-shirt, she headed out into her kitchen to get the coffee going. Her computer booted up as the coffee began hissing into the waiting carafe and she slipped into the chair, watching as the e-mails began to download. She didn't have too many to go through this time, just a handful, mainly from her editor and the publishing house, plus one from Sue. The dates for the release had been confirmed, along with a time and place for the party. It was a double celebration in many ways, both for a new release and the fact it was her tenth book with the company. That was a milestone she had never dreamed of reaching.

'Anything good?' he asked as he walked over to her desk. 'All I ever seem to get is junk mail.'

'Work related for the most part. I just got the one junk mail and one confirmation for the new book. It seems I have a party to attend in New York on the first of the month.' She tapped the screen as she explained. 'And I meant to say thank you for the roses.'

'You're welcome. I never really liked red roses to begin with, and I remembered you once mentioned in an interview that you preferred white roses over any others.' He nodded towards the screen. 'That's only three weeks away. Are you going to be able to make it?'

'Yes, I should be able to, and the book has been through its final proof so it should be heading for the printers on Monday. It wasn't due to be released until the following month, but sometimes books get bumped up.' She turned to look at him, still smiling from his comment about the roses. She couldn't help but wonder just how much more about her he knew and hadn't yet mentioned. 'I never like those parties, I'm always there with just the reps from the publishing house, my agent, and whichever editor I've been working with.'

'Sounds like you find it a little dull,' he commented.

'No, not dull exactly, just stressful. Everyone else is normally there with a close friend or partner of some sort. I'm used to being given the sympathetic looks by those who are in a couple. That "poor soul, I bet she writes these things because she's single" type of look.'

'And do you?' he asked, giving her a curious look.

'Do I write romance novels because I'm single? No, I write them because I enjoy writing them, though I'm thinking of trying a different genre for a while. I've been toying with the idea of a murder mystery set in London. All those Gothic buildings and the depth of the history over there gave me a lot of ideas, it's just that I really couldn't write over there. I kept hitting this huge mental block every time I tried.' She watched his eyes for some sign that he was just feigning interest in what she did. It was ridiculous; she was still expecting him to suddenly behave the way Andrew and others before him had.

'Would you have to write under another name if you did that? I'm not sure how these things work, to be honest. It's not a business I've had anything to do with, except as a customer.'

'I'm not sure. Fifteen years ago the answer would have been yes, publishing houses didn't like you using the same name for different genres. Things have changed, though, but it's something I really need to talk to Sue about.' She nodded towards the e-mail. 'Sue is my agent in New York so we only meet face-to-face about once a year.'

'This release party… I was thinking… that is if you would like me to… I mean, would you mind if I went with you?'

'Do you mean that?' He couldn't have surprised her more if he had offered to dance through the high street in a grass skirt and coconut bra.

'Yes, of course I mean it. That's if you'd actually like me there? I wouldn't want to push in where you don't want me to.' He shifted his weight from foot to foot as he spoke. She'd never seen him look as nervous as he did now.

'I'd love you too come with me.' She stood up and took

hold of his hand, smiling as she spoke. 'No one has ever asked if they could come with me before now. I was just a little surprised.'

'Then it's settled. All I need is a time and place. I can fly to New York with you or we can arrange to meet there. Either way works fine with me.'

He pulled her into his arms, holding her close. There was nothing sexual in his touch this time, no attempt to grab her hair or tease his fingers across her ass, just a strong and warm hug that held her cradled against his chest. She didn't try and kiss him, or spark any new play between them, instead she just relaxed within the circle of his embrace and closed her eyes.

'I can see why you love this place,' he admitted, turning them both enough so he could look out the window. 'It's peaceful… I think in many ways I had forgotten just what it was like out here.'

Hope soared and died in the same breath. 'But you have no intention of changing your mind about the building plans, do you?'

'No, I can't. I'm committed to this now,' he whispered into her hair. 'Perhaps I have made a mistake, but it's done now. I have a contract to complete if the project is given the go ahead that has been signed for months now.'

She wasn't sure if the regret she heard was real, or just a figment of her imagination and she was unwilling to press the topic any further. Sooner or later she would find a way that would stop the work from taking place, if she hadn't already with the annexation.

'What's that on the table, more notes for your work?'

'No, something else I was working on, and something I prefer we don't talk about right now.'

'Ah, then I presume it is something else to do with the lake project?' His grip loosened. 'We're going to have to talk about that sooner or later.'

'I know, I just don't want things to be spoiled between us. If we start arguing over the lake then I am worried it will split us apart when we've only just found each other again.'

'Why would it do that? You want the lake to remain the same, I'm interested in changing it, we both know where the other stands, so as long as we don't try to change each other's viewpoint we should be fine.' He was looking at the papers; she didn't need to see his face to know that.

'That I can agree to.' She slowly stepped back from his embrace to turn towards the papers. 'I was looking at local history, trying to find a reason to get the work halted. That's where I found out about the annexation. Do you know how it came about?'

'No, I wasn't even aware of it before the meeting,' he explained with a shake of his head. 'I've no idea why it wasn't mentioned to me before, and it could ruin everything.'

'Are you sure? No one mentioned it to you at all?' She looked closely at his eyes, seeking some sign of a lie.

'Not a word. I was as surprised as everyone else was to hear about it. How did it come about?' He moved towards the papers with interest.

'That's beyond strange.' She frowned and sorted through the notes and printed off sheets of paper. 'Here it is. It wasn't the normal reason for annexation, not how I understand these things, and I'll be the first to admit I don't really know much about this sort of thing. The land around the lake all the way into town, and three miles on the north side, was all originally owned by the same family. They discovered some deeds in the old Darvin house with the maps showing the lands they claimed and still held title to until the town of Darvin was chartered. Part of the charter reads that all the lands once owned by the Darvin family would be forever part of the township. All they did was annex lands that already were part of the town. The annexation just put it in modern legal form.'

'So it's always been part of the town?' He looked over the papers, frowning even further. 'So Baker wasn't doing his job?'

'That or someone bribed him not to mention it. I have to admit for a while I thought that person might be you.' She saw no point in hiding what he might well have already been thinking.

'And you don't now?'

'No, not any more. So the question is, who benefits from the project going through?' She sat down on the edge of the desk.

'First person I could think of would be my backer,' he replied. 'Except I'm not sure she would have the contacts to do it. She's not from this area, she just heard about the original project and contacted me, we moved on from there.'

'How did she find out? And isn't it odd for a woman to get involved in this sort of thing?'

'Not that odd, though I'm surprised you'd think so.' He grinned. 'I filed at copy at the State capitol, sometimes you get people contacting you from that. It can be a double edged sword though. You get equal amounts of hate mail and potential backers. This one worked out, though; she had the money I needed to expand the project. There was no way I could have financed something of that size on my own. The incident out at Battle Lake left me wary, so we agreed that she would front the money and put it into a secure bank account. I have enough there to do the majority of the work without having to dip into my own funds.'

He didn't hesitate in explaining how it all worked, which helped to ease the last of her concerns that he might have been involved. 'So she just came out of nowhere?' she asked. That sounded so odd to her that a stranger would come in from no where and offer him money.

'Yes, it's unusual, but it does happen. People with money, wanting to make more money who are looking for the right investment. In any other trade I know it would be looked at as if the money was automatically dirty, or there were other things going on, but in this trade it does happen. I wasn't expecting it to happen with me, or with this project, but it did.'

She shook her head, looking over the paperwork. She had papers everywhere, covering local Native American history to the storms all the way back until the late eighteen-nineties. 'Something doesn't feel right about this, Craig. How far did you check into the background of your backer?'

'I didn't have to this time. Once the money was proved to

be real the need to look deeply vanished. If she had been providing the money a little at a time then things would have been different. Besides, I'm a small operation, it's not as if I have the funds to do in depth research on people waving money at me. Yes, she could be behind it, but I doubt it. Honestly speaking this is more likely to just be some kind of mistake, an oversight Rob made.' He turned away from the paperwork at last. 'But if there is that annexation, then the plans will have to be redrawn and I'll have to give the backer the option of withdrawing. I'll know more about it when the report comes back.'

'A report. Do you know whose doing it?'

'More of an investigation, really. The Sheriff is overseeing it. You see, you weren't the first one to raise whispers about possible bribes. It's become a legal investigation.'

'What will happen if the investigation doesn't clear you?'

'That I don't know. I'm not sure I really want to think about that right now.' His mood darkened.

'And that would be because it could mean you being arrested?' The words slipped free before she thought enough to stop them. 'I'm sorry, I didn't mean to bring that up just yet. It's just that I had already thought about that possibility before we started talking about this subject. It's not something I want to see happen, so we need to find out just who else would benefit from this situation.'

The phone rang before either of them could say another word, which in some ways was a blessing.

'Hello?' she answered.

'Anita, I need you to come into the office as soon as you

can, I have some new information you really should look over. It doesn't look good for Craig.' Mark spoke rapidly, the words almost running one into the other. 'It's looking more and more as though he did bribe Rob to keep quiet.'

'I don't believe it, he wouldn't do something like that, Mark, you have it-'

'I don't have it wrong, the Sheriff just arrested Rob Baker for taking bribes and I don't see who else could be behind it. No one else has a stake in this.' He took a breath. 'Look, come down to the office and see for yourself.'

'Give me about thirty minutes and I'll be there, but you're wrong. I'm not sure what's going on, but you're wrong.' She quickly put the phone down before she lost the last hold on her temper.

'Mark?' Craig asked, his mood darkening even more.

'Yes, he wants me to meet him down at the office. He's found out something and he seems to think it implicates you in the bribes. Baker was just arrested for taking a bribe so-'

'So he thinks that, between the arrest, and whatever he's uncovered, I'm implicated in all of this.' He rubbed the back of his neck slowly. 'Then it might be an idea if I drive you back into town.'

Chapter Ten

They barely spoke on the drive into town. She had collected her research documents together in the space of a few minutes before they both headed for the truck. They had both made false starts with conversation only to end up finishing the journey in silence. At least he had been as willing to try as she was despite the stress they were both under. She had no idea what was going through his mind, but the thought of him being arrested for a crime she was now certain he did not commit only served to add to her determination to discover just what was going on. The lake had been bare of birds and boats alike when they had driven past it except for a lone heron at the north end. She had become so used to seeing at least one boat out there. It couldn't be that much longer until hunting season, could it? She had no interest in fishing or hunting and only remembered the season openings when she walked into a store in town and saw the notices posted everywhere.

The town was busier than she had expected when he pulled up outside the office, so when he let her out of the truck close to fifteen people saw her.

'I'll call you later today. Is that alright?' He leaned out the window as he spoke, but kept his voice down.

'That'll be fine. I'm not sure how long I'm going to be here, but I am hoping, seriously hoping, I can find out what's going on.'

'Will you be able to get to your car from here?'

'Sure, it's just a couple of blocks away.' She smiled as she tried to not let the stares she could feel on her back affect her too much. 'You best head off before we provide them all with something to gossip about.'

'Maybe I *want* to give them something to talk about other than accusing me of trying to corrupt a public official. But you're right, there's no point in giving them even more ammunition then they already have. Though they probably already have us wedded and bedded.'

'They'd be at least half right,' she replied, blushing. 'And I have no complaints about that at all.'

'Good, because neither do I.' He leaned further out the window, stealing a quick kiss from her lips. 'And they can talk, I don't care and neither should you.'

'Who said I did?' She winked before turning and nearly running into the office.

'So, do you really think it's wise you being dropped off by Craig?' Mark accused her as soon as the door closed. 'Or are you working for him now instead of me?'

Her jaw tightened. That had been the wrong thing to say and she barely kept her temper as she walked deeper into the office. 'I am not working for you, Mark, I'm working with you. I met him for the meal, he turned up on time, and what, if anything, happened afterwards is strictly no one else's business' She dropped the files on the cleaner of the two main desks. 'So what is it you wanted to discuss with me?'

Mark ground his teeth, but kept his comments to himself as he opened up the file he had been holding, spreading out the papers. 'Don't ask me where I got this, but it's something you need to see.' He pushed one of the papers into her hand. A photocopy of a check stared back at her, made out to Rob Taylor for five-thousand dollars from *New Vision Construction Funds.*

'I don't believe it.' She stared at the copy of the check, and even more so at the signature. 'Craig wouldn't do this, I know he didn't. I came outright and asked him. He told me he hadn't done this,' she protested, her throat tightening as she continued to stare at the signature. 'He told me he hadn't done this...'

'What type of criminal would turn around and confess to a woman he was trying to get in the sack with?' Mark snapped as he took the photocopy back. 'Or has he already managed that?'

'That's got nothing to do with this!' she declared. 'I believe him because it wouldn't make any sense for him to come into a town where half the people knew him and try to bribe a public official. He knows the area, knows how people here would react to something like that; he'd be digging his own grave. Why on earth would he destroy any chance he had to come home again?' She came so close to adding 'Or to come back to me' but what good would it have done? There was no proof he wanted to spend the rest of his life with her, she only had her feelings to go on and she was desperately clinging to the hope he had told her the truth.

'How about because he thought no one would discover what he was doing, Anita?' Mark retorted. 'He's arrogant enough to assume no one in town would be smart enough to figure out what had happened. That was always one of his biggest faults, his arrogance. I warned him about that back in school, but he would never listen. It didn't matter what he wanted, he'd go after it, and to hell with the consequences. He never even stops to apologize when he hurts a friend or a lover, you should know that better than anyone else.'

She struggled not to simply turn around and storm out of the office as he raged on about Craig. They were both as bad as each other, where one had gone the other had followed, and vice versa. Neither of them had seemed capable of admitting when they had done something wrong or had left a friend hurt, at least until now. 'He's changed, he's not the same person you knew, Mark.'

'Like hell he has. I've never heard him apologize for a single mistake in his life.'

'Yes, you have. After the meeting he apologized to me in front of you. He's been sending me flowers almost every day since I came home from England, even before we met face-to-face again in town. You're letting your personal feelings get in the way when it comes to Craig and it's about time you grew up enough to realize that!'

'How dare you-'

'If you bothered to take a moment to calm down and think you'd be able to see things a little more clearly. Craig has made a success of his life, Yes, he's still got a long way to go but he's getting there while you're struggling to keep the newspaper running. He's made no attempt to hide any problems he's had, but look around you, Mark, you're hiding just how bad things are for the newspaper from everyone, including yourself.' She gestured towards the flaking paint and damaged coat, the office that was empty of anyone other than the two of them. She'd kept quiet on a dozen small signs she had seen staring her in the face since she had walked into the office that first time. Even his drinking, to her, was an indication that things were going badly for him. 'And then there's your fixation with me, yet the only reason you keep making a play for me is because of Craig. You're not in love with me, you're in love with Lynn. I've seen the photographs.' She had watched the emotions play over his face, going from outright denial to shock and then quickly to outrage, until she flung the last accusation at him. The moment she said it she knew she was right.

Silence lay heavily over the room as he stared at her, small twitches moving his lips at random moments as if he was struggling to find a way to speak but he wasn't sure what to say to her. When he finally found the words his voice was tight and controlled. 'It would be best if you leave for a while before I say something we both regret.'

* * *

Walking through the town did nothing to help her calm down. The further she walked the more she thought about what had happened with Mark. She was right, she knew she was, he was letting his jealousy get the better of him. That foolish high school rivalry was still causing problems between a pair of grown men. If the situation hadn't been so potentially serious it would have been funny. There had to be a way to make Mark see just what a fool he was making of himself and turn his attention to finding out who was really behind the bribery. And that was where she had the problem. Unless he would admit to what was going on, and see that his interest in her was nothing more than a jealous streak, then there was nothing else that could be done.

At least she had been right about Lynn, except that only added to her growing frustration. They both were in love with each other, and neither of them had said a word about it to the person who needed to hear it the most. Worse still they both seemed to be keeping silent because of Mr. Gravy's problems with Mark. If they ever had the nerve to talk about their feelings then they might find a way to solve the problem with Lynn's father. Just what was his big problem with Mark anyway? She couldn't recall an incident that would have left him so biased towards Mark, but something must have happened.

Not for the first time she wished she had the ability to

turn back time and find out what had happened, but even trying to research it would have caused problems; she had nothing to go on. For all she knew Mark might have once knocked over a milkshake in a diner when he was a toddler and spilled it over Mr. Gravy and the man could have been holding a grudge ever since. It might sound ridiculous, but Ray Gravy was a man who held silly grudges beyond the point of sanity. She could remember a time when she had been in junior high. One of the smaller stores had short-changed him a penny, a single penny, and he'd raised hell about it. She could still picture him standing outside the store accusing them all of being crooks. As far as she remembered he had never stepped foot in the store again.

There had been some strange times when she had been growing up, but there had been some good days as well. The park had seen more than a few picnics, games of soft balls and evening walks. Darvin itself had changed a little in those years, but the core elements that she had grown to love had stayed the same, and now it all threatened to change, or it had until the check was discovered. Just how had Mark got hold of a copy of that to begin with?

The more she thought about the situation, the more frustrated she became. She was missing something, and it had to be fairly simple or it wouldn't be causing her so much trouble. That was how these things worked. The answer always turned out to be something so simple that she would kick herself later for not realizing it. She turned, walking back towards the parking lot of *The Red Deer* to collect her car. Craig had changed, Mark was just unwilling to see it.

Men! If they ever took the time to think things through then half the problems they encountered in life wouldn't appear to begin with. No, that was unfair, it wasn't just men who were guilty of that. She'd made her own share of mistakes and caused more than a few problems herself. It was just that Mark's ego was adding to an already difficult situation. If the two men could put their differences to one side then…

Then what? Everything would magically be fixed? The check would vanish?

'Slut!' hissed a woman as she walked past.

The accusation stopped Anita dead in her tracks. 'What did you just call me?' she demanded, turning to face the middle-aged matron.

'You're a slut, you always were and always will be. You don't even have the common sense to go to a different man this time, you just pick right back up with the same boy from school. We all know what you've been doing with that Dawson boy.'

'I beg your pardon?' She wanted to scream, to lash out at the woman for attacking her like that. 'What business of yours is it who I call a friend?'

'Oh, friendship is what they call it these days? And here was I thinking it was called sleeping around,' the woman snapped at her. She stared at her with a self righteous indignation that matched her all too perfect clothes. There wasn't a thing out of place on her except her hair, and even that could have been put down to the breeze. Her clothes were too expensive to have been bought in town, the earrings she wore might have come from New York, and her shoes weren't suitable for walking through a park. She almost looked as though she had walked out of a business meeting.

'Who I sleep with, and when, is my own concern.' Anita retorted. The woman had no right to walk up to her and treat her this way. Who did she think she was?

'Well I suppose I shouldn't be surprised with the sort of trash you write. It's nothing more than low-grade pornography. Your poor mother would turn in her grave.'

'And just how would you know what I write, Mrs. Warren, isn't it?' It had taken her a while to place the woman's face, but now that she had everything else fell into place. She had always been the one person you could rely on to lash out at others. 'How would you know what sort of things I write unless you've read them?'

Mrs. Elsie Warren turned a bright shade of pink as she sputtered out a reply. 'I would never permit myself to read that trash!'

'Then how can you possibly pass judgment on what I write without bothering to read at least one of the books through from beginning to end?' Anita took a step forward and jabbed her finger into the older woman's shoulder. 'It's people like you who give small towns a bad name. Instead of taking the time to learn something for yourself you're far more willing to attack others, to make assumptions and cast out insults to anyone in hearing range.'

'Well I never…'

'That's right, you've never thought much about anything. I might not be around that much these days, but I can well remember what you were like. You were a bitter cow when I was growing up and you're no different now, so get the hell out of my sight before I really lose my temper.'

With a look on her face that had to be a mix between shock and fear, Elsie turned and nearly ran.

How some people could be so vile she would never understand.

'Anita Burns?' Another woman's voice called out.

She turned, looking for the source of the voice, half expecting to have to fend off another set of nasty words. Instead she was met by the sight of a woman no older than she was with half wild mousy blond hair wearing a lime green t-shirt and pink sweats. 'Yes?' she asked warily.

'I thought that was you. It's Annie, Annie Bartlow. We were in school together.' The eager woman grabbed her hand and all but pumped it from her shoulder. 'Wow, you've hardly changed at all, you look so at peace with yourself. I guess it must come from writing all those wonderful romances. And good for you, sending that old hag packing, she always was a bitch.'

'Annie, you look different than I remember…' That was an understatement. The last time she'd seen Annie had been as the Home Coming queen, now the woman looked as though she'd not seen a brush in a week. How could the same woman who had been so vain in high school that she had checked her appearance in a mirror six times every hour, or so it had seemed, become a woman who most people would give a wide berth too? If her appearance wasn't enough to put people off, the smell coming from her certainly was. As far as Anita could make out, Annie hadn't bathed in several days, if not longer.

'I went on a retreat, has to be about six years ago now. I finally realized what a fool I was making of myself trying to dress to please everyone.' Annie laughed, the small lines around her eyes crinkling. 'I don't live locally anymore. I moved out to Wyoming. I came home two weeks ago on vacation, but I heard about those horrible plans that company had for the land out by your lake and decided to extend my stay to help with the fight. There's going to be a protest rally, isn't there?'

'No, I don't think so…' She was still trying to come to terms with the changes in Annie, but at least she was feeling better now that her mind had been taken off Elsie Warren's words.

'Why ever not?' Annie demanded. 'A good rally will stop them in their tracks.'

'I don't think that's going to be needed now.' Had Annie even looked in a mirror in the last few months?

'Oh? What's going on?'

'Rob Baker, head of the planning committee, has been arrested for accepting a bribe, so I think that will be bringing the whole business to a rapid halt,' she explained as she tried not to stare too closely at Annie. If she stood talking to the woman much longer she'd end up saying something about her needing a bath, or worse. 'Look, I don't mean to be rude, but I do have to go.'

'Oh, not a problem at all, I just wanted to say hello and let you know that I'm on your side. Well, where else would I be? I'm your biggest fan, after all. I have all your books and I tell everyone I can that I went to school with you.'

* * *

'Annie Bartlow, now there's a name I haven't heard in a while,' Conner remarked as he sorted through her mail. 'I had heard she'd moved out of State and thought I caught a glimpse of her the other day, but she looked so different. And I wouldn't worry about the Warren woman, she's always been a person whose found enjoyment in the misery of others. I'm very glad to hear someone finally put her in her place.'

'That's one way of putting it.' She tried not to shudder as she replayed some of the accusations in her mind. 'I've been dealing with accusations about my writing most of my career, or so it seems.'

'There will always be people who can't separate fact from fiction. Strange thing is you don't hear about many horror writers or writers of murder stories being accused of being murderers in order to be able to write about those things, do you?'

'No, and I doubt you'll ever hear much of that type of accusation, it's just ridiculous, but the minute you write something with a hint of sex in it, especially if you're a woman, you must be someone who's writing from experience. If you write romance then you're secretly looking for love. I write both, so I get it two-fold, and those same people would profess to be intelligent.'

'Well you know what you're like, so I wouldn't let them get to you.' Connor pushed the small pile of mail across the counter towards her. 'You still look pretty shaken there, Anita, is there something bothering you? You're not still worried about the building work out at the lake are you? I'd heard that had been put to rest with Baker being arrested like that.'

'It's Craig,' she admitted with a small shrug.

'Ah, yes, prime suspect in the bribe scandal, though I can't ever believe the boy would be behind something like that. It's just not in his nature. He's done some stupid things in his life, haven't we all, but at heart he's a good one.' He leaned on the counter, watching her closely. 'But then again you'd know that better than most, wouldn't you?'

'Yes, I guess I would. Half the town knows about him and I, then?'

'No, I'd say it was closer to everyone in town, and most of those in the surrounding areas as well.' He was only half joking. 'News travels fast in this part of the world, but the good part is that it's often just as quickly forgotten. This time next month you'll be old news.'

She could only hope that was true. 'At least I'll get a small break from all of this mess next month.'

'Ah, yes, the book launch, isn't it?'

'Yes, that's right. I'll be in New York, if all goes well. I don't suppose there's much that happens in town you don't see or hear about eventually?'

'That's part of the job description.' He chuckled. 'I see everything, maybe not as soon as would be helpful sometimes, but what I don't see, I hear. People have this odd habit of stopping and talking to me when they come to pick up their mail. You've done it yourself on more than one occasion.'

'Like now,' she replied before putting her mail to one side on the counter. 'Can I ask you something?'

'Sure. Ask me anything you like. I'm not saying you'll like the answers you get, though.' He nodded.

'Do you remember what happened to cause the break up between Dawson Senior and Mr. Gravy? What happened to split them up as business partners?' It was a long-shot but the only chance she had to try and put some of the pieces together. If she could figure out why Lynn's father didn't like Craig then maybe she'd also discover why he didn't like Mark, and at least then Lynn and Mark might have a chance together.

'Yes, yes I do. That was some time ago, over twenty years if I remember right. They'd been working together for years, doing repair work, building small projects together, they even worked together on the new town hall.' He took a moment to think before continuing. 'They'd not long finished working on it when old man Dawson turned greedy. He had a chance to go for a big contract in Hayden.'

She nodded as Conner mentioned the town twenty miles away, storing away the information in case she needed to take a trip out there. 'What sort of contract?'

'Twelve new houses and an extension to the school. It would have brought him in a lot of money and he wasn't happy about sharing it. He didn't involve Gravy in the deal, kept him completely out of the loop until it was too late and the contract was signed with only Dawson's signature on the bottom. It wouldn't have been too bad, but the arrangement between Dawson and Gravy had always been a verbal one, so when Gravy tried taking him to court to get his share of the money he didn't have a case. The judge threw him out, awarded everything to Dawson. That would have been the end of the matter, but Gravy spent the next two years in and out of court trying to reverse the decision. By the time it was all over he didn't have a penny left to his name.'

'I don't understand... if the family had been bankrupted wouldn't Lynn have been left with nothing?'

'I didn't say the family was left with nothing, Gravy was. His wife was one smart cookie, she had her own funds, money she kept well out of his reach. Can you imagine what it would have done to a man like Gravy to have to live on his wife's charity? I don't doubt she rubbed it in every chance she had. It only made things worse when the Paper ran in depth coverage of all the cases. Lloyd Taylor just loved painting out every lurid detail of Gravy's stupidity.' He shook his head. 'You know, pride is a terrible thing, and Gravy has enough of it to keep five men happy.'

Her head was pounding as she tried to sort through the new information. 'So Gravy has never forgiven Mark for something Mark's father did?'

'I can't say for certain, but it would sound about right for him.' Conner admitted. 'It would be in keeping with his character traits, as you might say.'

That, at least, got her to laugh, but it didn't ease the headache that still threatened behind her eyes. 'The path of love did run smooth...'

'Ah, then you know about Lynn and Mark?'

'Damn, you don't miss anything at all, do you?' She laughed, rubbing her temples.

'It would be a little hard to miss when she always finds a way to steer the conversation towards him,' he admitted. 'As for him, well he avoids her name and any mention of either her or her family as if they were plague infected. Men only do that for two reasons, and one of those would be love. Men are strange creatures, and I can say that honestly with being one.'

She smiled a little at his words and leaned on the counter. 'Well, I know Craig isn't responsible for bribing Baker, the question is, how do I go about proving it?'

'Try going directly to the horses mouth,' he suggested.

'Baker?' she queried. 'But he's in custody.'

'True, but there's no harm in trying, and who else would know who handed him the check?'

As much as she didn't like the idea, he was right. If she wanted a chance to prevent them from eventually coming after Craig, she had to find out the truth.

Chapter Eleven

'You want me to let you just walk in and talk to someone we've arrested? When did you become an attorney?' Sheriff Johnson walked out from behind his desk and fixed her with a hard stare.

'I never claimed I'd become anything of the sort, and I knew it was a long shot, but I had to ask. He's the only one who can say who gave him the money.' She tried not to wish the floor would open up and swallow her. 'Look, I know Craig isn't behind all of this and if I can do anything to help prove that, I will.'

'You might want to be careful how you phrase things, Miss Burns, that could have been construed as an attempt to bribe me.' He spoke plainly.

'What?' She took a step back, replaying the words in her mind. 'I never implied any such thing.'

'The word "anything" can be taken to mean just that. Now, I know you didn't mean it that way, but I would have thought that a woman like you would have phrased things a little more carefully. If you know what I mean. Now, you should also be aware that I cannot let the prisoner have any visitors just yet, not unless it's his attorney. He's not been before the judge yet and when he is, that will change.'

'I just hoped… I just need to find out who is really behind all of this,' she said as she sat down hard in a wooden chair.

'Well, I don't like saying this, but maybe you have misplaced loyalties on this. Young Craig isn't the best person in the world for you to be seeing right now.' He rested his hip on the corner of his desk as he spoke. 'Now I know you care a great deal for the lad, I'm just suggesting you might want to put a little distance between the pair of you. It would be far too easy for you to end up caught in the middle of something that is more than likely going to turn as nasty as hell before the end of it.'

It wasn't that simple, she couldn't just walk away from the man she loved, and she did love him, she knew that now. There was something about him that made her feel at peace with herself. 'I can't just walk away from him, Sheriff.'

'You can do anything you have to or need to do, Miss Burns. I would strongly advise you keep your distance from Craig Dawson until all of this is cleared up one way or another. I wouldn't want to see you caught up in the middle of all this, it might not be a very good move for that career of yours.'

She nodded, unable to reply with the way her throat had tightened. The day had gone from being wonderful to a mess.

'It's been one strange day, that's for sure. Between dealing with this case, the usual fallouts from weekend parties, and a pair of panties that had one woman up in arms when she found them in the park, I'll be very glad when I can honestly call this day over.'

'Someone found a pair of panties?' she nearly choked on the question as she tried to keep her cheeks from burning.

'Yep, a pair of black satin panties from last night, I expect, expensive by the looks of them, but probably some teenager took them from her mom's closet to impress the boyfriend,' he said, but the look he was giving her didn't quite match his words and only added to her growing discomfort. 'You know how kids are.'

'Not really, but I'll take your word for it.' She got to her feet. She had to get out before he asked her about the blush that she was sure now covered most of her face. 'I should go, and thank you for being so honest with me.'

'Not a problem, I'm just glad you took the refusal so calmly, it makes a nice change from people barging in here and shouting at me, demanding their rights. Of course most people have no idea what it is they can actually demand, and forget they'll get a far nicer response if they just ask me.' He walked her towards the door, and then leaned forward to whisper in her ear as she walked out. 'And next time you decide to explore a little healthy fun somewhere, you might want to remember to pick up everything before you leave.'

Her cheeks were still flaming by the time she walked the three blocks to her car. If she had been able to keep herself from reacting the Sheriff might never have known the panties belonged to her. Now she would never be able to look him in the eyes again without blushing. She tried telling herself it could have been worse, that he could have discovered them in the park when she and Craig had been leaning against the tree.

It had already been a long day and it wasn't over yet; she still had to get her car and head back to the house. Not that she expected to find any new answers there, but with Mark angry the only place she could go work was home. Perhaps she should have followed Craig home last night in her own car, but she had been enjoying the feel of his arms about her body far too much to think about that.

'Anita?' a familiar voice sobbed out the word.

'Lynn?' she asked as she looked towards her car. There, leaning against it, was Lynn, her face streaked with tears. Her hair was a mess, and she appeared to have been crying for some time. 'What on earth happened?'

'It's pop… he got so mad at me I thought he was going to hit me. I've never seen him like that before. He was swearing at me, throwing things… I got so frightened I had to leave. I can't go back there, I just can't!'

Anita stood for a moment in the parking lot, holding Lynn tightly against her as she tried to make sense of what had happened. 'We can't just stand around in the parking lot, and if I take you back to my place your father will find you all too easily. I'm hoping he doesn't come on my land, but I also wouldn't put it past him.'

'I know, that's why I didn't just go and hide out there. I've no idea what to do. I ran out without even grabbing my wallet.' Lynn was shaking even though there was no sign of her father. 'He just exploded when we were talking. He started yelling that I was an ungrateful slut.'

That decided it for Anita, she wasn't going to let that man get anywhere near Lynn. It wasn't the first time Mr. Gravy had upset Lynn, or treated her like little more than dirt under his feet, but as far as she was concerned it was going to be the last. 'Right then, I'll take you where he won't think to look for you.'

* * *

'There you are, you forgot to give me your copy for the Paper? Is it all ready to go?' Mark stopped in mid sentence when he noticed Anita wasn't alone. 'What's going on?' he demanded as she brought Lynn into the office. 'Lynn? Are you okay? You look like you've been crying.'

'That's because she has been,' Anita replied as she made sure the door was closed before urging Lynn to sit down next to Mark's desk. 'Her father exploded on her, frightened the hell out of her from what I can see and what little she's said.' Lynn was still half crying as Anita explained what had happened. 'No one deserves to be on the end of that sort of abuse.'

'Abuse?' Lynn gulped. 'I never said he abused me, Anita. I

said I was afraid he would hit me, he never has, though. It's just his temper that had me frightened, and what he said to me.'

'Lynn, you don't have to be physically assaulted in order for it to be abuse. Shouting at you, degrading you, always keeping a track on where you are and what you're doing, controlling any part of your life, calling you names when you do or say something he disagrees with, that's also abuse.'

Lynn looked up, glancing from Mark to Anita, and then back down at the floor. 'He's not that bad,' she tried to protest, but the words lacked any real conviction. 'I just thought if I kept quiet about it he'd mellow out one day. Normally I'll try and keep the peace, avoid topics I know set him off, I just let my mouth run away with me today, it's really all my fault.'

'No it's not. You can't let yourself think that way. What would you tell me if my father was still alive and had left me a crying and shaking wreck?'

For a moment there was silence before Lynn finally replied in a soft and still shaking voice, 'I'd tell you to get the hell out of Dodge,' she admitted.

'Then take your own advice for once. You have two friends here who are not going to let him get to you,' Mark spoke up as he stepped around his desk to sit in front of Lynn. He reached for her hands, taking them gently in his. 'I've never wanted to see any harm come to you,' he added gently.

Anita smiled as she watched the light dawn in Mark's eyes, a silent admission of what he felt for Lynn, or so she hoped. It wasn't a proposal, or a declaration of love, but it was a good start, and exactly what Lynn needed to hear. As she stepped back to give the couple a little room, she could see some of the tension ease from Lynn's shoulders. 'What set him off this time?' she inquired once she saw Lynn had stopped shaking.

'It was a discussion about Craig. I knew he'd tell me to shut up, but I came home from picking up some groceries and he was all but prancing about the kitchen singing that Craig was going to be arrested, and how the only way his day could get any better is if they announced that Mark was joining him in the cells.'

Anita frowned. Some of this wasn't making sense. 'Craig hasn't been arrested, Baker has, and how would he know that Craig might end up having a warrant sworn out on him? It's not written in stone yet. I don't think the Sheriff has enough to move against him.'

'I don't know… maybe someone called him from town and let him know what was going on. With my pop you can never really tell half the time.' Lynn wiped her face with a tissue Mark handed her as she tried to think things through. 'It did strike me as odd, though, and I told pop he was wrong, that Craig had nothing to do with it. That's when he started yelling at me how could I know, everyone had thought Dawson was a good man and look what he did, that sort of thing.'

'Dawson… he was talking about Craig's father?' Mark inquired, still holding on of her hands gently in his. 'Why would he be talking about Dawson Senior? He's dead.'

'I think I know what he meant. I spoke to Conner today; he

filled me in on some of the things that had happened with the partnership break up. Craig said his father wasn't the good man everyone thought he was, and it looks like he was right. It would seem that he cut your pop out of a good chunk of money some years back.' She sat down on the edge of the second desk as she watched her two friends. 'He's never forgiven either Dawson Senior or your father, Mark, for the trouble they caused him.'

'My Dad, what has he got to do with all of this?' Mark demanded.

'Apparently his coverage of the court cases that followed where less than glowing when it came to Mr. Gravy,' she explained.

'That would explain why pop would never even buy a newspaper. I couldn't even mention it existing. He said a few years ago that he would sooner set fire to the whole place than ever buy a copy,' Lynn offered in a quiet voice. 'I'm sorry if my pop has caused more problems for everyone. I just wish he would grow up and let me get on with my life.'

Anita was silent as she worked through some ideas in her mind. Lynn needed a safe place to stay, but she was reluctant to suggest she stay with Mark. Not that she thought he would take advantage of Lynn, from the way he was looking at her he was more likely to stand watch over her through the night than lay a finger on her. 'What if we got Lynn a motel room in town and gave the Sheriff a heads up about the possible situation?'

'That might work, or she could stay with me,' Mark offered almost shyly. 'That's if you'd like to?'

'Yes, yes I would.'

Mark might not have realized it but she wasn't just saying yes to staying with him for the night but for the rest of her life, except the only one who probably realized that was Anita. Still, she wasn't going to spoil things for them both. 'If you two are sure about that then I'll leave you to it. I need to head home for the night. It's been a long day and I am in dire need a good cup of coffee.' Well she was in dire need of something with the way the day had been going, but one look at the soft smile on Lynn's face at least helped to chase away some of the lingering doubts she might had had about leaving her in Mark's care.

* * *

Her head was pounding when she pulled off the main road and down the lane towards her house. With everything that had been going on she had barely had a chance to breathe let alone stop somewhere to grab a cup of coffee, so in one way she had been telling the truth, she did need one in the hopes it would ease the headache stubbornly sitting behind her eyes. She hadn't realized just how late it was, but by the time she got into her car to drive home it was already nearly five o'clock.

The large red Ford pick-up truck barreled around the last corner before she could pull into her driveway, forcing her to swerve out of the way as it sped out of sight. It was only when she turned and swore at the retreating vehicle that she realized it was Ray Gravy's truck.

'That bloody man, he could have killed me! If he's been in my house I'll have him arrested for breaking and entering!'

She turned the car into her drive. What was it with that man? Did he think he could do whatever he pleased without having to deal with any consequences?

Another vehicle, one that was almost familiar, sat waiting for her just outside her barn, but this one was a far more welcoming sight. 'Craig!' she sighed in relief. With him there she doubted the older man had got past the front door, which was a blessing, but it would have also given Gravy yet another reason to hate the younger man. By the time she got out of her car Craig was out of the house and walking towards her.

'I guess you saw your almost visitor?' he called out as he hurried closer.

'He almost sent me off the road. He's mad, or he simply doesn't care about anyone other than himself.' She stepped into his open arms. Just being near him made her feel alive and desirable. She could feel the outline of his cock pressing against her body through his jeans as she leaned upwards and wrapped her arms about his neck.

'A little of both, I suspect. I didn't think you'd mind me coming here to wait for you. I can't do much in the way of work until everything's sorted, and with them arresting Baker it's only a matter of time before they find out who bribed him. Then I can get back on with my life, though I am betting I'll be looking for a new project.' He spoke into her hair as he held her close. 'As for Gravy, he came here looking for his daughter. When I wouldn't let him inside he stood there ranting and raving for over twenty minutes before he finally just snarled some warning at me about watching my back and drove off.'

'Lynn ran from him. I met her in town. He'd lost his temper with her and she didn't feel safe staying home any longer. I managed to calm her down a little and she's staying the night in town.'

'That sounds like the safest thing for her. Gravy always has had a temper on him, it's one of the few things my dad and I agreed on. That man never lets go if he thinks he's been slighted.'

'She's going to be staying with Mark,' she added, watching for his reaction.

'Well that sounds like a good idea. I know he and I don't get on, but he won't let anything happen to her. I'm hoping things settle down between us in the coming months.'

'So do I. These have been a difficult few days for everyone concerned.' How could she tell him there was a check with his signature on it made out to Baker? All she wanted to do was rest against his chest and breathe in his scent. Well, maybe not quiet all she wanted. Still there was no point keeping it from him. 'It might not be that simple to just try and forget the things still waiting for us back in town, Craig. I think someone has been trying to frame you.'

He turned them both towards the house, one arm settling about her waist as they walked inside. 'What do you mean?'

'There's a check, made out to Baker, with what looks like your signature on the bottom of it. I saw a copy of it, and it's not going to be long before the police find out about it.' She looked around the kitchen, her gaze settling on a large vase that sat on the counter filled with what looked like two dozen white roses. 'Oh…'

'A check? How could there be a check to Rob? I never wrote one to him and never authorized anyone else to write one. The only two people with access to that account are me and the backer, and I would have seen if someone had drawn a check on the account. I did a daily check on the balance just to be on the safe side.'

'I don't know what to say then, Craig, except that the flowers are beautiful. I never expected to come home and find something like this waiting for me.' Somehow with everything that was going on thanking him for the flowers seemed out of place. 'It looks like you've been busy.'

'I had planned on cooking you a meal but Gravy turning up spoiled that, or at least delayed it.'

'Aren't you worried?' she probed, trying to understand him.

'About the check, yes of course I am, but there's no point in me stressing out about something I can't do. My bank isn't a local one, and I have no way of contacting them until tomorrow as the office will be closed now.' He hugged her close for a moment. 'I'll call them first thing in the morning to try and get this sorted out, you have my word on that. In fact, you can sit in on the call if you want and listen for yourself.'

'I don't need to do that, I trust you.' She tried refusing the offer.

'I do want you to listen in. I know you trust me, but that doesn't stop you from having some doubts. Listening in might stop that.' He pushed her back a little but still kept her within his arms so he could look down into her eyes. 'I do love you and I don't want anything to happen to spoil what we're starting to build between us.'

'So there's nothing that can be done until tomorrow morning?'

'Not unless you know of another way to contact the bank and find out who issued that check?' He smiled as he pressed his lips softly to hers.

Even if she had known of a way she was more interested in responding to his kiss than speaking at the moment. She pressed upwards, her lips parting under his at the touch of his tongue. A tingling moved across her skin, surging into her nipples, turning them into hardened pips under her blouse as she pressed against his body. He grasped the back of her head, caressing her hair, tangling his fingers in it before he deepened the kiss. With a soft moan she accepted his tongue's entrance between her lips.

'I want to enjoy this time with you,' he murmured, letting her go to walk into the kitchen fully. 'It might sound strange but I still want to cook that meal for you. That's if you'll allow me to do that?'

How could she refuse a man who wanted to cook for her? She had never been the most skilled of cooks and often lived on quick meals, omelets and cereal, pieces of toast grabbed on the way to the computer along with the occasional piece of fruit. For the next hour she sat on one of the bar stools, watching as he prepared a meal, pan-frying two tender pieces of steak in red wine, slicing up mushrooms and carrots tossed into the pan once the steaks were removed. He spoke of simple things in life, cooking meals for a family, taking road trips, spending time walking along a beach with the woman he loved, about things that made her heart sing and worried her at the same time. There was something soothing in his words, his plans, the dreams he had for his life, and it was something she wanted to be a part of.

They carried their food out onto the deck, lighting candles to keep away the mosquitoes so they could eat without any extra guests joining them. She didn't say much as they ate, content for the most part to listen to him speak and immerse herself in a daydream. It wasn't easy to shut out the worries she had for him, she had seen the check, but she tried.

'What do you think will be said when you show up with a date for the launch?' he asked, leaning back in his chair once the last of his dinner had vanished from the plate.

'I'll get twenty questions from Sue, but other than that it depends on what members of the press are there. There isn't quite the same amount of interest shown in established writers than there is with say the new flavor of the month,' she explained as she looked out over the lake. 'It would be a little different if I turned up married, but even then the reaction would be low key. I'm nowhere near the top ten or even one hundred authors of the country. Perhaps one day I will be, but not right now.'

'What would you do if you hit the top ten in the bestseller list?' His tone was wistful.

'You mean other than faint?' She smiled; it felt right somehow discussing dreams with him. 'Celebrate, throw a party, then get right back into writing.'

'Is that it?' He frowned and looked at her more closely.

'What else did you think I would do, it's not as though it would get me anything. It wouldn't give me a grant or award and it wouldn't keep me in royalties long-term. I'd have to go back into writing just to be able to keep those who read my work happy… That sounded a little big headed didn't it?' She almost laughed.

'Not really. I think I understand, you only get to the top by writing good books, and you only stay there by continuing to write good books.' He leaned forward, taking hold of her hand. 'And I believe you do write very good books indeed, Anita.'

Her gaze lowered to the table as heat crept across her skin, his fingers tightening on hers just enough for her to take notice. 'Thank you.'

'I mean it.' He let go of her hand and got to his feet, picking up both of their plates before he walked back into the kitchen. 'Stay right there, I'll be back out in a minute.' He was as good as his word. 'I was wondering if you would like to take a walk around the lake with me,' he said.

'I'd love to.' Smiling, she stepped away from the table and into the circle of his arm. They didn't talk during the walk down from her house to the water's edge, nor did they exchange more than a few words during their stroll along the beach. She didn't feel a lack in the silence, if anything, she welcomed it; it felt comfortable, settling, after the busy day she had had.

'I can see why you like this place,' he echoed his words from that morning as they stopped in a sheltered part of the beach where the wind couldn't quite reach them as anything more than a slight breeze. 'And I'm not that disappointed about the contract falling through. Let's be honest, it *has* fallen through. Even when I'm cleared no one will want to see it approved, there will be too many bad memories associated with the idea.'

'I can't say I'm upset about that either,' she confessed. 'Though I wish it had fallen through in a way that didn't call your character into question.'

'It will all be sorted out, trust me on that one. I'm innocent, that will be proven at the end of the day.' He stepped in front of her, pushing a finger under her chin, lifting her gaze to meet his own. 'I love you, Anita. That isn't going to change and we will get the chance to explore that, if you want to?'

'I do.' She smiled back up at him. 'I want to spend the rest of my life with you, if you'll have me. I don't know why, and there's a part of me that says even though I've known you for years this is happening too quickly, that I should wait and see what happens in the coming days, but I don't care anymore.'

He leaned down, brushing his lips softly over hers, whispering against them as his hand pressed into the small of her back, 'I've was a fool when I left you here, I was a bigger fool when I almost destroyed something that means so much to you, but I don't want to ever be a fool again when it comes to you.'

'Marry me?' she asked, tears stinging her eyes.

He smiled, his gaze never leaving her face. 'I can think of nothing else I would rather do than become your husband, my beautiful, talented and spirited Anita.'

Chapter Twelve

'Somehow I always thought it was the man's job to ask the woman to marry him.' He smiled as he spoke. 'Traditionally it is, yes.' She turned her head enough so she could brush her lips over his palm. A part of her couldn't believe he had said yes. She'd been shaking inside when she'd finally asked him, and when he had said yes the relief had been intense, like a rush higher than any orgasm she had ever experienced. 'But it felt right to ask.'

'I'm glad you did…' He gasped as she nipped at the tender skin of his palm, his eyes going wide when her lips moved away to catch his finger. 'You're a very wicked woman.'

'Yes, I am.' She grinned, the words mumbled with his finger in her mouth, but she wasn't satisfied with only holding the tip. Her tongue wrapped about his digit, suckling as she eased her lips down. Was he imagining she had her lips wrapped around his cock? She suckled harder on his finger, licking around it, scraping her teeth over his skin as she slowly drew her lips back to the tip.

'Maybe you should be using those wicked lips elsewhere?' he asked with a low groan. 'You keep that up and I'll be forced to carry you back to the house over my shoulder and toss you onto the bed.'

'Why the does it have to be the bed, why not the floor, or couch or even the table in the kitchen?' she suggested, and tried to capture the tip of his finger again.

'Oh that's it!' In one quick move he lifted her over his shoulder. She couldn't help but laugh when she found herself hanging down over his back. Even though her hair blocked her view she knew he was striding towards the house. She knew, and she loved the thought of every wonderful thing they might get the chance to do together. 'You're mine, Anita, I'm going to make love to you until you scream for mercy.'

'You say that as though it's a bad thing!' She laughed, trying to spit the hair from her mouth as she placed her hands against his back and pushed up. The light smack to her ass caught her off guard, pushing a yelp from her lips. 'What was that for?'

'You're my captive and you can stop struggling, wench!' he declared playfully. 'I've fought through endless hoards to capture you as my prize.'

'Have you been reading too many romance novels?' she taunted, and was about to continue when she felt his hand slip between her thighs. 'Oh!'

'No, but maybe I should read a few more if I'm going to be

a convincing rogue who comes to carry you off to serve his dastardly desires.' He pushed open the door into her house. 'Do people actually use that word any more?'

'Which word?' she gasped out the question because his fingers where still pressed between her thighs and now brushed against the soft fabric of her panties.

'Dastardly.'

'No!' She tried not to squirm.

'Ah, I'll try and remember that.' He shifted her down onto the table, laying her on her back. 'Now you look far better to eat than any food I could possibly imagine.'

She laughed and tried to roll free, only to feel him capture her thighs.

'Now now, I didn't say you could go anywhere, did I? Yes, just the thing to satisfy the hunger I can feel growing, though I would say you are a little overdressed right now.'

She didn't get the chance to answer; he had already reached up and yanked her panties down only to toss them out of sight.

'That's an improvement, but we have a long way to go yet.'

Her skirt was bunched around her waist, baring her pussy to his view, but he wasn't satisfied with that and reached for her blouse. With rapid tugs he pulled it open and tossed it to the floor. His hands reached for her breasts, still covered within the cups of her bra, massaging them with slow, firm strokes.

She whimpered, her nipples hard under the cloth and his hands, her back arching as she caught her bottom lip between her teeth. The straps slipped from her shoulders, the cups tugged down, freeing her breasts to his eyes. Her nipples had become hard points as the skin around them crinkled in anticipation of his touch, goose bumps covered her body, and her gaze never left his face.

'I can't believe you're doing this,' she murmured, her back arching again as his lips claimed one hard nipple and his fingers captured the other. With a low moan she writhed on the table as his tongue flickered over the trapped flesh between his lips. His fingers pinched her other nipple, rolling the tight flesh between them, tugging in time to the rapid flicks his tongue playing over its twin. Each flick, each pull and tug, elicited a low whimper from her as her cunt clenched in rhythm.

'I plan on doing a lot more,' he warned around her nipple, tugging it gently. 'Don't hide your responses, love, I want to hear each moan, each whimper, your groans, even your pleas. I want to know every part of you, your deepest desires, hopes and fears.' He wasn't even touching her clit yet it still throbbed with his words, her hips pressing forward to meet the hand that wasn't there. Her thighs parted wider, her knees bending as she set her heels against the smooth wood of the table top.

He devoured her breast, suckling, licking, nipping at the soft white skin, tracing his tongue over its stiff peak, dancing over it. Her teeth caught her bottom lip, her back arching further as her hands grasped the edge of the table above her head, her hips rocking upwards, her thighs tightening and releasing with each inner spasm that claimed the walls of her wet pussy.

Slowly he moved down from her breasts, licking a path between them over her ribs, tickling lightly only to trace a circle around her naval. Her nipples throbbed from the lack of his touch, a throb her clit eagerly reflected as she pressed upwards with her hips in a silent plea, and yet still he didn't touch her there.

'Eager wench, aren't you,' he teased as he traced his tongue across her body from hip to hip. 'You want me to delve between your thighs, to taste you, to take your clit into my mouth and press a finger between those wet lips…'

'Yes' she whimpered.

'Soon,' he promised. 'Very soon, you just need to be patient.' His hands grasped her thighs as his tongue left her body, parting them wider.

She groaned when his lips touched her ankle, tracing a wet path with the tip of his tongue around the small bone. What was he trying to do, set every nerve-ending on fire with the need to feel his cock buried inside her? She wanted him, needed him, to fuck her but he'd made it all too clear that would happen only when he was ready, and not before. Her thighs tightened in response to his tongue running along the inside of her thigh, tracing so close to her pussy, but still not touching. 'Please Craig, please…'

'Please what?' he asked, blowing across the lips of her vulva.

'Touch me!' she begged.

'I am touching you.' He moved closer to her pussy until she could feel his breath playing across her tingling skin.

'Touch my cunt,' she pleaded, arching her hips towards him. 'I need you to touch my cunt!'

'I know,' he replied in a way that made her want to scream in frustration. She could feel him so close to her sex, so close to touching her clit, to parting her lips and sinking a finger slowly inside her. Was he going to leave her to wait even longer? She cried out in delight as he brushed his fingers over the lips of her sex, parting them slowly and blowing gently over her clit. Her hips arched upwards, her finger tightening on the edge of the table as she pressed towards his face. Without any further teasing he captured her clit between his lips, circling it with his tongue before sucking gently on it. Small beads of perspiration formed on her breasts, her lips parting, and moans became cries when he pressed two fingers slowly into the depths of her clenching sex. She rocked down against his hand and lips, seeking out the delights he offered, clenching, tightening and releasing on his fingers as his lips held her throbbing clit in place. Her thighs tightened, her body no longer felt as if she had any real control over it, as though it had become an instrument for him to play. With a deep groan she pressed down onto his hand, grinding down against his fingers. 'I could lick your cunt for hours!' he growled into her clit.

Hours… she couldn't take hours of this, not when she wanted to feel his cock inside her body. 'Please, just fuck me, Craig.'

'Is that what you really want?' His tongue circled her clit relentlessly, his fingers pressing deeper inside her body to tap against her hidden spot.

She cried in delight as he tapped again and again, each touch within her freeing another cry from her lips. She didn't know where one wave of pleasure ended and the next began and each one pushed her higher than then one before. With a strangled scream she half sat up on the table, grasping his shoulders, her nails digging into his skin. Her cunt tightened fully on his fingers, her hips pressing down as he wrenched an orgasm from her. A pleased growl vibrated through her vagina as he pulled his fingers out and gently pressed her back against the table only to tug her hips forward until her ass rested against the edge of the wood. She trembled as the spasm's played through her body, barely hearing his clothes hit the floor, only realizing what he was doing when she felt the head of his cock press between her labial lips. He waited only long enough for her to register what was happening before he thrust into her tight pussy. She cried out, arching upwards to meet his thrusts, rocking back against him willingly. Her hands pressed to the table as she half sat up and wrapped her legs around his hips. She ground down around his cock, her lips finding one of his nipples. His hands held her hips, his thrusts pushing deeper and deeper into her body. Tight spasm's rocked from her cunt to her clit and up into her nipples.

'Come for me,' he commanded.

'Yes!' She gasped the word. Her body was still tingling from the first orgasm he had given her. Her fingers dug into his skin, she bit into his shoulder as she cried out, and still he pushed upwards into her cunt. He wasn't going to stop, it didn't seem to matter that she had come, he kept fucking her with all his strength. 'Please, come for me, come for me, Craig!''I'm going to…'

'I love you!' she cried out.

'My Anita!' he groaned, his cock pulsing against the walls of her pussy as he thrust one last time, his fingers digging into her hips as she felt cum surging deep inside her…

* * *

His fingers played through her hair as he held her close. She could barely remember him lifting her from the table, but he must have done as she knew her legs were still trembling; walking would have been impossible. Now she rested half in his lap as they nestled together on her couch. Her clothes were still somewhere in the kitchen, but he had pulled the soft fleece throw from the back of the couch to wrap around them both.

'You're a wonderful woman, Anita,' he whispered against her cheek.

'No, I'm not,' she protested, leaning against him.

'I think you are. You've stood by your beliefs even though they went against plans I had and still I can't stop myself from being in love with you. Not that I would want to.' He brushed a soft kiss against her cheek. 'I'm not planning on ever leaving you, unless you tell me to go.'

'That might not be a decision we have a choice in,' she commented, trying not to think about what would happen if they couldn't prove he was innocent.

'I think I turned you into a hot and sticky mess.' He smiled, brushing back the hair from her face. 'And it's not that I'm complaining, but would you object to sharing a shower with me?'

'Now why would I have a problem with that?' The thought of him pressed against her, their bodies wet and slippery, had her clit throbbing already. It wouldn't matter if they only helped each other clean off, she'd be content with that; she'd still enjoy the feel of his body close to hers. 'I think that's a wonderful idea.'

'It's agreed then.' He said as he pushed to his feet, his arm curling around her waist as they walked towards her bedroom. 'Though I think you're just about ready to curl up and go to sleep on me. Anyone would think I 'd worn you out or something.'

Heat crept across her face. 'Maybe you did.'

'Well in that case you'll have to remind me to do it again.'

Steam curled upwards from the bath as he turned the water on. He stepped into the stall, offering her his hand to help her in, catching her when she nearly lost her balance. She wasn't used to sharing a shower with someone, but she wasn't going to turn the experience down. 'Or maybe next time we can relax in that hot tub of yours out on the deck?'

Either idea sounded wonderful to her. 'Perhaps we can do both?'

He laughed and reached for the soap. Her eyes drifted closed beneath his touch, his hands working into her hair as the scent of the shampoo reached her. She leaned back against him, the water hitting his body first before spraying over his shoulders onto her skin, his fingers working firmly into her hair and scalp. She could have stayed that way forever, just standing in the shower with him as his fingers seemed to find and hit every right spot in her scalp and neck. 'Enjoying?' he inquired.

'Yes,' she murmured, her eyes remaining closed.

'Good.' He slowly turned her around, slipping past her so she could feel the water hitting her body fully.

She sighed as the water rinsed the soap from her hair and body, taking a moment to work in some conditioner before she reached for him. 'It's my turn now.' With slippery fingers she worked the soap over his chest, brushing her fingers across his nipples with a playful tweak.

They were still laughing by the time they curled into the bed together. They'd always been able to laugh together, even when they had been teenagers, and it was something she had missed in other relationships. 'I think I've always been waiting for you to come back to me, Craig,' she admitted.

'That doesn't sound like such a terrible thing,' he replied as he closed his eyes and pulled her against his side. He yawned, tugging the blankets about them both. 'Just as I've wanted to be able to fall asleep with you in my arms ever since I left town. Wanting that doesn't make us bad people.'

'No, I guess it doesn't.' She agreed, watching his face. She knew he was tired, and though she was as well, she wanted to watch him for a while longer. 'Go to sleep.'

'You'll get no arguments from me there…'

Just how long she lay there watching him sleep she doesn't know, but eventually she too fell asleep resting within his arms. After all, this was where she was meant to be.

* * *

'Did you want some coffee?' he asked as she stumbled into the kitchen, blushing at the sight of her clothes still scattered across the floor. 'I was about to make some anyway.'

'Sure. You're up early.' She bent to pick up the clothes. The clock had barely read seven a.m. when she'd rolled out of bed in search of him. She'd searched the bathroom, stopping long enough to wash and pull on a pair of jeans and sweatshirt before walking out into the living room. The relief she felt when she had realized he was still there had been enormous. She couldn't help the doubts that continued to plague her, though they were dissipating with each new challenge that was overcome.

'I tend to wake up early; it's a normal part of the job at construction sites. There are some days I've been on site by five o'clock, others I have worked until nine at night. It all depends on the deadline, the light and the type of work I'm doing.'

'That makes sense.' She tossed the dirty clothes into the basket. 'Did you sleep well?'

'Like a log.' He smiled and walked over to her, wrapping her into a tight hug. 'What about you?'

'Very well, indeed.' She wasn't quite ready to admit she had spent some time watching him. 'I was a little worried when I woke up and you weren't there, but that was just me being silly, I know that now.'

'With everything that has been going on no it's not that silly at all.' He held her close to his chest and brushed a hand down her back, cupping at her ass. 'It's a lot to go through and I'm sure once I make that call to the bank a lot of this will be sorted out.'

'When will we be able to put the call in?' she inquired, breathing in his scent.

'Soon, another hour or so and there should be someone around, and once we get that sorted out it will be a lot easier. The stress will ease up and we can start focusing on more important things, like finding you a ring.'

'Do you think they'll be willing to talk to you over the phone like that?' She wasn't sure how security on these things worked.

'They might, if not I'll have to sort out another way of doing this as it's too far to just drive there and get back in a day. With everything that's happening we need the information quickly. Perhaps I can get the bank here to work with them or see if I can do a teleconference call with them. Either way, this will be sorted out.' He gave her a quick squeeze before releasing her. 'It sounds like that coffee is ready and we could both do with a cup.'

She followed him into the kitchen and sat down at the breakfast counter. 'I could get used to this.'

'To what?'

'To having someone around who cooks and gets coffee on, though Lynn does a wonderful job of looking after me. There've been times I doubt I would have remembered to eat if she hadn't driven by. She's been a great friend to me over the years, and I hope she and Mark finally get something sorted between them.'

'Ah, then you've noticed. Mark has had a thing for Lynn since high school, he just never said anything about it. Not that I blame him with the way her pop is. He'd have done everything possible to stop them getting together. At least now she's old enough to make her own choices.' He handed her the mug. 'That man needs to learn to leave his daughter alone, but I doubt he will ever do that.'

She took a sip. 'He might in time, but it's a long shot, I agree. I can see her just having to accept that he will never approve of who she wants in her life.'

'And does she want Mark?' He settled down on the stool next to her, still naked from the waist up.

'Yes, I know she does. To be honest, I think she's been in love with him for as long as you say he's been in love with her. I never really noticed until she mentioned something the other day, but she's always kept up on what he's been doing, asked me how things where at the Paper, that sort of thing.' She wondered if the signs been there all along. Not that it mattered now, they had both admitted in their own ways that they cared for each other, and the rest would be for them to figure out between them.

Craig frowned and looked out of the window, setting the mug down on the counter. 'It looks like you've got company.'

She followed his gaze as he slipped down from the stool and pulled on his shirt and shoes. Two cars were pulling up in front of her house, both from the local police department. Her heart sank as she watched Sheriff Johnson step out of his car and walk towards the door. 'Anita, can I come in for a few?' he asked through the storm door. The look on his face was grave and he held a piece of folded paper in his hands.

'Yes.' The word almost stuck in her throat. She didn't want to let him in but saw no point in saying no. As much as she wanted to hope otherwise she already knew why he was here.

'Thank you, I'll try and do this as easily as I can. I'm sorry.' He turned his gaze towards Craig before handing him the paper. 'Craig Dawson, I have a warrant for your arrest on the charge of bribing a public official. You have the right to remain silent, if you give up that right to remain silent anything you say can and will be used against you in a court of law.' He reached for the cuffs as he began to read Craig his rights.

'No,' she protested, taking a step towards the two men. 'He's not guilty of this, he isn't, you have to believe me.'

'Anita, stay back. I have to do this and I don't want you to get into trouble by trying to stop me. Craig, turn around, I have to put the cuffs on you. Just procedure, I'm sure you understand that.'

'I do.' He turned, putting his hands behind his back. 'Don't try and stop him right now, Anita. We'll fight this in court. Phone Greg McCollum, he's been my family's attorney for years and I still rely on him for contracts and other details.'

'I will. Sheriff, why are you arresting him now?'

'Baker confessed that Craig gave him the bribe and told us about the check. The bank provided the rest of the details.' He secured the cuffs in place. 'I warned you to keep your distance from him, Anita. I'm sorry it came to this, but I can't just ignore what he's done.'

'I'll follow you down.'

'There wouldn't be much of a point in doing that. I won't be able to let you see him. The only one other than myself and my officers who will be getting anywhere near him until he goes before the Judge will be his lawyer.'

She nodded, not trusting herself to speak anymore. All she wanted to do was lash out, grab Craig, somehow free him from the cuffs and run, but what good would that do either of them? He was innocent, she could prove it, would prove it, somehow. Her hands clenched when the Sheriff led him out from the house. She followed them as far as the front step, watching them take the man she loved to the squad car. She didn't move, couldn't move even when they drove off. Her legs felt like lead, her stomach churned itself into a tight knot as she fought not to be sick. Only when the cars had disappeared from sight did she let herself cry....

Chapter Thirteen

He was gone, she couldn't believe the Sheriff had simply turned up and arrested him when she knew he wasn't guilty. He couldn't have done it, she knew that. It wasn't how he was. She turned and ran into the kitchen, tears stinging her eyes as she fought to breathe. She tried focusing, taking slow breaths as she leaned against the counter. It wouldn't help him if she curled up in a ball to cry or looked for things to throw no matter how tempting both options felt. There had to be something she could do.

Greg McCollum, he had told her to call Greg.

She scrambled for the phonebook, flicking through the pages as she searched for his name and number. It might be too early for someone to be at the office, but she could at least try. She scuffed the tears away with the back of her hand and reached for the phone.

No answer. She'd have to try later; it wasn't even eight yet. Most of the offices in town wouldn't be open until nine, but she couldn't just sit around and wait. She had to find something to do. She picked up the phone again, but this time dialed Mark's number.

'Hello?' Came the sleepy voice on the other end of the line.

'Mark, it's Anita, they've arrested Craig.'

'I said they would,' he mumbled. 'What time is it anyway?'

'A little after seven. Look Mark, I need your help, they arrested him here, he's not guilty. We were going to call his bank and find out what had happened. You have to believe me, he didn't do this.'

'Okay, okay, I believe you. They arrested him out there… what was he doing at your place this early…? Oh, I see. Okay. Are you all right? I'm sorry, I didn't really think about how seeing them arrest Craig like that would make you feel.'

'I'm a bit shaken. I never thought they would do that.' She frowned as she half heard another voice on the other end of the line but couldn't make out what was being said. She'd hoped for more time, a chance to clear his name before it reached this point.

'I can understand that. Look, we'll be out there shortly. Just stay calm and we'll figure this out together. I don't want you driving anywhere on your own right now, I'm not sure you'd be focused enough to be safe on the road.'

Her hands were shaking by the end of the call. Mark was right, getting behind the wheel of a car right now wasn't the safest think for her to do, but she couldn't just sit there and wait for Mark and Lynn to turn up. She paced the kitchen, her mind a whirl as she tried to think. The attorney would have a better idea what to do, but she couldn't get hold of him for at least another hour.

She hurried into the bedroom and tidied it up, tugging the bedding straight. Her fingers played over the pillow he had used and without thinking she hugged it to her body, rocking as she sat on the edge of the mattress. Fresh tears stung her eyes, the knot in her stomach tightened as she lost her grip on her fears. They crashed down on her as she sobbed into the pillow, every dark thing she could imagine playing through her mind. Craig sent away for years, being killed in prison or simply never being released. Could she handle years without him now that she had accepted just how much she loved him? Worse still was the dark voice that suggested he was guilty and that he had been lying to her the entire time. Her fingers tightened on the pillow as she rocked, trying to focus on his scent that still lingered on the material, to cling to the hope that everything would somehow work out. She wasn't being rational, she knew that, but it didn't stop either the tears or her fears.

Time lost meaning, her throat growing raw from the sobs that shook her shoulders. Only the distant sound of a car pulling up in front of her house sobered her up. Shaking, she dropped the pillow onto the bed and hurried into the bathroom to try to scrub the signs of worry from her face before she walked into the kitchen.

'Anita.' Lynn hurried over, enveloping her friend in a tight hug. 'I'm so sorry, really I am. If there's anything I can do to help, I'll do it, you know I will.'

'I know,' she replied, trying hard not to cry again. Tears wouldn't help, and she didn't want her friends to think she couldn't cope. 'He didn't do it.'

'I know. Even Mark knows, though he's being an ass and not admitting it.'

'I'm not being an ass, I'm just trying to be objective.'

'If he'd done it he'd have fled when Baker was arrested, or found a way to cover his tracks instead of being out here with the woman he loves,' Lynn declared.

'I guess, unless he was trying to make the police believe he had nothing to hide,' Mark suggested.

'Mark! Use your common sense, you've known him for years, he's just not like that.' Lynn let go of her friend and turned on him. 'Stop being such an ass and think about this.'

'All right, you win, he's not guilty. Now can we get on with it? Does Craig have a lawyer?'

'Yes, he told me to call McCollum in town.'

'He's a good man, my Dad used him on more than one occasion. He should be in the office by now. Do you want me to make the call?' He walked towards the phone.

'Please, I'm not sure I can think straight just yet. They arrested him on charges of bribing a public official.'

'Okay. Lynn, take her out onto the deck, or find something to help focus her. We'll need to figure out what we're doing once I finish speaking to McCollum.'

Anita obediently followed Lynn out onto the deck and walked to the railing, leaning against it as she looked out over the lake. 'I'm trying not to think of all the things that could go wrong.'

'I can't imagine it's easy for you.' Lynn followed her out to the railing. 'I wanted to thank you, though.'

'For what?'

'For taking me to Mark. We did a lot of talking last night. I think we got some things sorted out between us. I never knew he even liked me, let alone loved me.'

'He told you that?' She turned and looked at her friend, seeing the warmth in Lynn's eyes, a confidence and happiness that nearly shone from her.

'Yes, he did. I know it's too soon to think about anything more than dating and getting to know him, but I think we have a chance for something very special between us and that wouldn't have happened unless you'd taken me to the newspaper office when I ran from pop. I doubt I would ever have had the nerve to tell him how I felt without you doing that.'

'It was just the right thing to do.' At least Lynn and Mark had a chance even if she didn't… No, she had to stop thinking that way. Craig would be fine, they'd clear his name, or McCollum would.

'Did pop come out here looking for me?'

'Yes, but Craig was here and sent him packing. He nearly ran me off the road. I swear that man is insane. I know he's your pop, and I know you love him, but he's crazy.' She looked back out over the lake.

'He doesn't think of anyone other than himself,' Lynn admitted. 'I'm not sure what mom ever saw in him. I know they were in love, I know they argued, and I know she never left him, but other than that...' She sighed. 'I've lied so much to myself and others about the way he is, the way things were between him and mom, just because I wanted to believe he was a good person, but he's not. I'm sorry he came out here looking for me, but I think we both knew he would try that.'

She didn't want to put Lynn's father down to Lynn, but she couldn't keep quiet. 'I'm glad you've seen what was going on, Lynn. I've known for years that you weren't happy at home, but I didn't want to lose the friendship I had with you over your pop.'

'I understand that. I'm not sure how I would have reacted a few years ago, even a few months ago.'

'Okay, McCollum is going to be waiting for us down at his office,' Mark announced as he walked out onto the deck. 'He's going to find out as much as he can before we get there, though he did warn me he won't be able to discuss a lot of what he finds out, there's that attorney client privilege.'

'That makes sense.' Anita stepped away from the railing. 'I'm not sure I'd be able to think straight even if he did try and tell me.'

'Lynn, it might be best if you ride in with her. I still don't think she's safe to drive alone yet, and we might need both vehicles at some point.'

* * *

'Where did you get a copy of the check, Mark?' Greg McCollum inquired. He was an older man; he had to be around sixty-years-old, but even though his black hair was dotted with grey his eyes were still bright.

'A friend, and one I don't want to get into trouble.'

'Well I've known Craig for years, I have copies of his signatures on file and this looks close, however, I'm no handwriting expert which is what we need here. Also, I've known him for a long time and he has an odd quirk of signing forms with one particular pen. This looks different somehow, but a good lawyer will argue he just used the one he had handy at the time.' He shrugged and put the photocopy into his files. 'It's a place to start.'

'So you believe he didn't do it?' Anita asked.

'Yes, though if I did or not he's still my client and as such I can't discuss any further details of the case with you. I will also be going down to the town jail to speak with him shortly. I'm not sure how long it will be until he's arraigned. It would depend on when they can get the Judge in.' The town had its own small courthouse, but it was rarely used for anything more than handing out fines. 'Judge Harvey has a habit of sleeping in late.'

'Will he be able to get bail?' Mark asked.

'Yes, though he'll need someone to post it for him.' McCollum looked directly at Anita.

'I can do that. I have some savings, and I still have all the money from the past couple of advances.' She had learned to keep careful track of her money for emergencies, but she had never expected to have to cover anything like this. Still, she had enough, or believed she would have even after the trip to London.

'Good. I'll need to contact the bank and find out when this was cashed.' He looked at the date on the check and frowned slightly. 'Something isn't quite fitting into place here, but I can't put my finger on it yet. When I find out anything, I'll be in touch. Until then I suggest you three go and get something to eat, then go through whatever other notes you may have. If anything comes to light, contact me.'

'Mr. McCollum, please, can you let him know I believe him, and that... that I love him?'

'You have my word on that.'

* * *

The hours crept by as she waited in the newspaper office for word from McCollum. Conversation had long since died between the three of them. She wasn't sure how many times they had attempted to talk about general things, from the weather to sports, but their hearts weren't in it. The idea of food had just turned her stomach and she'd already drunk more coffee than she normally did in two days.

'We can't just sit here doing nothing,' Lynn protested finally.

'I know,' Mark agreed, 'but I'm just not sure what else we could do. We've been through every scrap of information in the office. Until we hear back from McCollum we have no idea what the next step is.' They had even tried calling Craig's bank, but it had done no good. Without a signed power of attorney there was nothing the bank could do to help them.

'This is frustrating,' Lynn exclaimed. They had searched

through every filing cabinet in the office, but had found nothing that might help them with Craig's case.

'Agreed, but it's a waiting game, that's all we can do, just wait for him to arrive.' Mark shrugged and sat on the edge of his desk. 'Damn, it's not even noon and I feel like I've been up a full day.'

'I know what you mean.' Anita rubbed the back of her neck. 'How long do you think it will take?'

'I don't know, but if it takes much longer we'll call the Station and find out what's going on,' Lynn said firmly.

'And we'll be lucky if they give us the time of day. The Sheriff made it very clear there would be no point in me following Craig down to the station as he wouldn't let me near him until after the arraignment. Apparently the only person who can see him is McCollum.'

'Great, so we go back to-' Lynn broke off as the door to the office opened up. 'Mr. McCollum!'

The older man smiled as he walked in. 'That took a little longer than I had expected, but I needed to fax a copy of some paperwork to his bank. I'm also getting a copy of the check sent to a handwriting specialist I know in the cities,' he filled them in as he pulled out one of the chairs and sat down.

'How is he doing?' Anita asked as Lynn moved over to stand with Mark. 'How's he holding up?'

'He's doing well, he's remaining calm and co-operating fully with the investigation, which might well help in the long run. He'll be going before Judge Harvey in an hour.'

'That soon?' Mark asked from where he stood with his arm around Lynn.

'It's one of the advantages of a small town. The Judge doesn't have anything else on the docket, but there's a chance he might have to pass the case over to the county. However, that won't happen until after Craig's been granted bail. Judge Harvey is not going to pass this case up without good reason, and for no other reason than because it offers him a change of pace.'

Anita almost laughed at that. 'Do you know how strange that sounds? The case saved from being moved because the Judge is bored of the current workload.'

'Yes I do, and it's not something you'll hear about often, so we'll take advantage of it. I suggest you be at the courthouse in forty minutes, no later. I'm not sure how long the hearing will take, but it's just a hearing. If you haven't eaten, do so. These things can be stressful and I don't want either ladies passing out because of lack of food.'

* * *

They had eaten, but it had been hard work for all of them. The food had been hard to swallow, even for Mark, who normally had a veracious appetite. But with a burger in each of them, and yet more coffee, they settled down in the small courthouse and waited for the Judge to appear. The building was little more than four rooms and a public toilet.

'Remember what I said,' McCollum told them, 'if you can avoid it don't speak directly to the Judge. If he speaks to you, stand up in order to answer and be polite.'

'Preaching to the choir here,' Mark quipped.

'I'd prefer to be on the safe side by making sure everything is understood than risk Craig being refused bail because of a mistake.' He fixed Mark with a hard stare. 'You aren't exactly known for your ability to keep silent. I believe the last time you attended a court hearing the Judge in question had you fined for contempt?'

Mark had the good grace to look embarrassed as his gaze shifted to the floor of the hall. 'I lost my temper, it won't happen this time, my word on it.'

'I'll hold you to that, Mr. Taylor.' McCollum nodded. 'When we go into the courtroom I'll be at a table on the left-hand side, Craig will be brought out to stand with me during the hearing. I doubt he'll be removed from his cuffs. Don't let that upset you, it's a small courtroom and there may not be enough deputies around to justify him being uncuffed.'

Anita took a slow breath, trying to calm her nerves as they walked between the double doors into the largest room in the building. Two rows of benches sat behind a simple railing with a gap in the middle for people to walk through. Two dark-wood tables sat in front of the railings and beyond that was the large raised desk of the Judge. They weren't the only ones to enter the room. They had barely sat down when three men entered followed by Mr. Gravy.

'What's he doing here?' Mark hissed.

'Perhaps he's come to see the show.' Lynn leaned closer to him. 'He must have had a call from someone in town about this. There's no way he'd miss a chance to see Craig shown up. I bet more than a part of him is hoping you say something and end up in trouble as well.'

The doors opened at the side, bringing the conversation

to an end as one of the Deputies escorted Craig in, still in cuffs as they had been warned. Only when he was in place and the acting Prosecuting Attorney stepped up to the other desk did the Judge finally walk in.

'The charges are bribing a public official, namely one Rob Baker, in the attempt to illegally obtain permission to build properties at Lake Crane.' Judge Harvey read from the paper the Sheriff had handed him. 'How do you plead, Mr. Dawson?'

'My client wishes to enter a plea of "Not Guilty" your Honor,' McCollum replied.

'I see, and is your client expecting to be released on bail?'

'Yes, your Honor.'

'And why shouldn't I believe your client isn't a flight risk? He has properties outside of the county, even the State. His roots are no longer with this community, or at least that's the argument I'm expecting from opposing council.'

'That's correct, your Honor.' The nervous-looking young attorney spoke up for the first time. He took several breaths, swallowing hard as he attempted to appear more confident than he apparently felt. 'Our initial investigations into Mr. Dawson's background indicates he's an extreme flight risk, with access to large sums of money, including the very same funds which he drew on in order to commit the act of bribery.'

'That would be the alleged bribery,' McCollum corrected calmly.

'Pardon?' The young man queried, shifting his weight a little, his feet shuffling over the polished wooden floor of the courtroom.

'It's still alleged bribery, unless you are under the impression that my client has been found guilty.'

'Mr. Nigel is quite new to appearing in court, Mr. McCollum, so has yet to settle in completely. However, I am quite sure that when this case is brought before me it will be one of his more senior colleagues who will be arguing the case for the prosecution.' Judge Harvey smiled.

'Yes, your Honor,' Mr. Nigel replied sheepishly.

'So, Mr. McCollum, just why should I feel comfortable with releasing your client on bail?'

'Because I have it on authority that Mr. Dawson is engaged to one of the residents of this county.'

'I see, and that would be our resident celebrity, Miss Burns?' He looked towards Anita. 'Well, Miss Burns, has the defendant agreed to marry you?'

She stood before answering. 'Yes, your honor, he has.'

'I see, and would you be willing to give assurances to the court that he will remain in your care?'

'Yes, your Honor,' she replied without hesitation.

'Then Mr. Dawson you are here by released on bail and that bail is to be set at forty-thousand dollars, cash or bond.' The gavel slammed down onto the desk as he closed the file. 'The date for your next court appearance, Mr. Dawson, will be sent out within the next week, and I will see you gentlemen then.'

She could barely stand still as she waited for the cuffs to be taken off Craig. Only then was she allowed past the table and into his arms. She tried to control herself, to stop the shaking from showing as she held him tightly. 'It's going to be alright,' she told him. 'I just have to go and pay the bail and I'll be right back.' It was only when she turned that she saw the pure hatred in Mr. Gravy's eyes.

Chapter Fourteen

'So, I've been released into your care?' Craig smiled as they stepped out of the courthouse. It had been nearly an hour before they were finally able to leave. Between the paperwork she'd had to fill out and running back and forth from the bank, it had taken far longer than she had expected. At least now that was over and she had Craig back with her for the time being. So they had to wait for a court date to be set, but that would give them the time they needed.

'Yes, you have, for now, at least, so I guess that would mean you'll have to stay with me out at the lake, just so I can keep an eye on you.' She smiled, leaning into him as they walked out of the small building.

'I will see you tomorrow, nine o'clock sharp, Craig.' McCollum smiled and shook his client's hand. 'By then I should have some word back from my handwriting expert. Once we have that we'll have a better understanding of where to go from there.'

'Thank you, Mr. McCollum. I appreciate your help in all of this.'

'I'm just doing my job.'

'I'll go and get the car,' Mark said, 'then we can decide what we'll be doing next.''Well then, what shall we do with the time we have?' Craig asked, giving both Lynn and Anita a teasing look. 'One man alone with two lovely women, that sounds like heaven to me.'

'Craig Dawson you behave yourself,' Lynn chided. 'I wouldn't class being in the middle of the high street as being alone, would you? And besides, you're engaged. And don't you have something important to do, like buying Anita a ring?'

'Or enjoying the last few days of freedom you have?' a new voice added.

Anita didn't have to turn to know it was Ray Gravy.

'They should never have released you out on bail, Dawson. But you won't be out for long. I always knew you were as bad as your father. He was nothing more than a lying cheating bastard, too. I didn't get the chance to see him in jail, but I'll be throwing a party when they lock you up.'

She could feel Craig's fingers tightening on her arm. 'Have you quite finished?' he asked, far more calmly than she knew he felt.

'No, not by a long shot, Dawson. You've had this coming to you for years and I'm damn glad I'm going to be there to see you destroyed the way your father destroyed me.' He snarled, taking a step closer to them. 'And as for you, Lynn, I'd better not see you anywhere near my home again. You've turned into nothing more than a slut spreading your legs for that idiotic newspaper man.'

'Pop, you need to calm down. Your words can't hurt me anymore. I've stopped caring about them,' Lynn replied in a low, steady voice. 'And from what I understand, wasn't it your own fault that you went broke chasing endless court cases in the name of revenge?'

'And I suggest you be very careful what you say to me, Ray, before you open a book one day and find your own name staring back at you from the pages.' Anita stepped out a little from Craig's embrace. 'There's an old saying, the pen is mightier than the *sword.*'

Whatever reaction she might have been expecting from Ray Gravy it certainly wasn't him bursting into laughter. 'Oh, Anita, you have no idea just how mighty the actions of a pen can be. Or signatures.' He turned and walked away, still laughing. 'You'll soon find out just how much his signature is worth.'

Lynn stared blankly after her father.

'I wouldn't worry about him, Lynn,' Anita said. 'We all know your pop has real problems with Craig, he's just blowing steam.'

Lynn shook her head.

'What's wrong?'

'I don't believe it,' Lynn murmured. 'I just don't believe he would stoop that low!' She turned, looking at Craig. 'Craig, you're backer, what's his name?'

'Why?' he demanded.

'Just tell me. What's the name of your backer?'

'Eileen Wright,' he replied, staring at her hard.

'That bastard, that bloody bastard! I never believed he would go this far. He's behind this! Eileen Wright was my grandmother's maiden name, and the signatures, Anita, do you remember I said he'd been practicing what I thought was calligraphy?'

'Yes.' Her mind was racing as she looked from her friend to Craig and back again. 'He wouldn't have, couldn't have! Didn't Conner say he'd been left bankrupt by the incident with Craig's dad?'

'Yes, but he has to have raised the money somehow. It can't be the house, I'd know about that, it's in my name, mom made sure of that. He has a small stipend paid out monthly to him from a fund mom left for him, but the rest of it went to me, and my account is fine.' Lynn was pacing now, but then she stopped and started walking towards the police station next to the courthouse. 'We have to get hold of the Sheriff.'

'What?' Craig demanded as they followed her, trying to keep up. 'Why?'

'She's right, if we head out to the house without the Sheriff involved Ray Gravy can claim we planted evidence. Everyone knows you've been right here under the care of the Sheriff. I was with you last night, Lynn was with Mark, her car still here in town. If we get them to search his stuff now no one can accuse us of planting anything,' Anita explained breathlessly as they all but ran into the Station.

'I need to see Sheriff Johnson,' Lynn demanded. 'And I need to see him now.'

'He's in the back taking a break,' the young Deputy replied.

'Then he can get off his damn break and get out here now, before it's too late. I think I know whose behind the bribery. Whose really behind it! And if he wants to be able to get hold of the evidence before it vanishes then he needs to get out here now!'

* * *

'I can't believe he would go that far,' Craig muttered as he and Mark and Anita sat in the car. 'It's as though he let his hatred take over his entire life.'

Lynn had driven in with the Sheriff, the three of them following behind in Mark's car. They'd been given strict instructions not to move from the car and had only been given permission to follow on the grounds they did exactly what they were told to do. Until the Sheriff stepped back out of the Gravy home and gave them the all clear, they were not to leave the car.

'It happens with some people, an overriding compulsion to get revenge even if they attack someone else instead of the person who actually caused the harm in the first place.' Mark watched the house intently. A warrant hadn't been needed as long as Lynn was present and had given her consent for the search.

'What do you think they'll find?' Craig spoke quietly.

'I'm not sure, Lynn didn't say much, but I think she knows more now than she was letting on. How long have you been in contact with this Eileen Wright?'

'All in all about three months now, before I came back home, but only just. It takes a while to sort these things out.'

'Between working on signatures, raising money, setting plans in place, making sure he could offer a bribe to Baker, he must have been planning this for months. He may well have had another plan in place before this one.' Anita rubbed her fingers against her temples. 'I've never met a person with that amount of hatred in their hearts.'

'He would have needed a copy of my signature, which he would have got from the contract I signed with him. Except I signed that in person and met Mrs. Eileen Wright.' Craig frowned. 'This has to be a wild goose chase.'

'No, not it's not. He could easily have hired someone from out of town to play the part for a while, or he might have someone involved in this as a full accomplice.' She spoke quickly. 'It's been done before. I remember Sue sending me some clippings from a New York paper about an actress being hired to play a role in order to con someone out of a family inheritance.' The story had turned her stomach at the time, but she'd kept the clipping as a possible idea for a story line in later years.

'Do people actually do that?' Mark asked incredulously.

'Yes, some people are sick enough to pull things like that. Truth really can be stranger than fiction.'

Lynn and the Sheriff had been in the house close to twenty minutes now, and there was still no sign of them. Silence settled in the car as she slid over the back seat to lean against Craig. His arm curled about her waist, pulling her to him.

'I can't imagine what this must be doing to Lynn,' she murmured. 'To find out that your father is behind framing someone else for a crime and for no other reason but revenge.'

'She's stronger than most people give her credit for,' Mark commented.

'And when are you popping the question?' Craig teased as he turned a little in the back seat to let her lean more comfortably against his chest.

'You might want to let me get my feet into this relationship before you expect me to ask her to marry me.'

'If you hurt her Mark…' Anita began to warn him.

'I am not going to hurt her, I just don't want to rush into marriage. Yes, I love her, but after this she's going to need time to figure out what she wants in life. I don't want her to feel as though I'm pressuring her into anything.'

That made a lot of sense to her, and she had not suspected that Mark could be that sensitive until recently.

'I'd prefer to wait until the time is right.'

'You never know, Mark. She might pull an Anita and ask you instead of waiting for you to ask her.' Craig chuckled. 'I have to admit, when Anita did that it was the best surprise anyone has ever given me. Of course, it would have been better if she had gone done on one knee to do it. She didn't even have a ring ready for me.'

'It looks like they are coming out now,' Mark said tensely as he craned his neck looking at the front door. 'Yes, they're out and there's the all clear sign. It looks like they've got quite a few boxes and files. It's not looking good for Gravy, I think.' He stepped out of the car as Mark and Anita quickly followed him.

Lynn waved and started walking towards them as Anita turned, hearing the sounds of a truck making its way back up the driveway. 'Shit, her pop's here!'

The red Ford barreled towards the house, barely stopping before Ray Gravy jumped out of the cab. 'What the hell is going on here? Johnson, explain what's going on, have you been in my house?'

'You're daughter gave her consent for us to search the house,' Sheriff Johnson explained calmly.

'She had no damn right, this is my house, my home! She's nothing but a little slut and I kicked her ass out.' Ray Gravy declared as he rounded on his daughter.

'She had every right to give consent to the search as the house belongs to her, not to you, Ray. I'm well aware of the terms of the Will as far as the house was concerned. Your wife had me witness her Will when she changed it to make Lynn the benefactor.'

Gravy turned and charged towards his daughter. 'You stupid little slut!' he growled, his fists clenching. 'You've never understood what I went through, you never respected me, not like a daughter should.'

Mark had moved faster than any of them, putting himself in between Lynn and her father.

'Keep your distance,' he warned quietly.

'Or you'll do what? No, that's not your style, is it Mark? You're like your piss-ant father, you're far more likely to write some scathing little story about me just like he did.' He took a step closer to Lynn and Mark. 'And you can keep the worthless little slut. I don't want to ever see her step foot on my property again.'

'Perhaps you weren't listening, pop.' Lynn kept calm as she spoke. 'As I've known since mom died, and just like the Sheriff pointed out, the house belongs to me, not you. I've never pushed the point home with you before, but if you think I'll stand here and let you order me off land I own you are even crazier than I thought you where.'

'You ignorant little bitch!' he snapped, raising his hand.

It wasn't the Sheriff, or Lynn, who intercepted the blow, it was Mark who stepped fully in front of her, blocking the her father's hand with his arm, giving the Sheriff time to move in and grab Ray's arm.

'You can't go attacking your daughter like that, Ray, you should know better.'

'Let me go!' He struggled against the grip of both the Sheriff and one of the Deputies. 'I've done nothing wrong!'

'You're under arrest, Ray Gravy, for attempted assault on your daughter,' Johnson stated as they worked to get the cuffs on him. 'You have the right to remain silent.' The words where lost as Ray spit curses at the Sheriff, Mark, Anita, Craig and Lynn, but especially Lynn. They were vile words, hurtful, aimed to tear into his daughter and degrade her, but Lynn kept silent as they forced her father into the back of the squad car and locked the door.

'Are you all right?' Anita asked once the door was closed. Lynn had turned pale, her bottom lip caught between her teeth.

'No, but I will be.' Her quiet voice was strained. 'It will take a while, but I'll be fine.'

'I know you will be, but you're not going through this alone.' Mark pulled her into his arms, holding her tight. 'I won't let you go through this alone.'

Craig turned, watching the Sheriff walk over. 'It looks like the Johnson wants a word.''Yes, I do. Lynn, thank you for letting us search the house. I can't comment on what might happen as yet, we have to go through the items you let us remove. As for your father, he'll be kept in custody overnight and I'll be advising he be charged with attempted assault. I think it would be best if you apply for an Order of Protection.'

For a moment Anita thought Lynn might argue against the suggestion, but instead her friend nodded. 'I'll be there in the morning, Sheriff, thank you.'

* * *

'Lynn is holding up better than I would have done if it had been my father,' Anita admitted as she watched her friend walk to the washroom in the small diner. 'I'm not sure I'd have been able to stand up to him the way she did.'

'I don't think most people ever realized the amount of strength that Lynn has within her. I certainly didn't until recently,' Mark said with a proud smile.

A minute later, Lynn walked back to the table and slid

into the booth next to Mark. 'Well, I think I've just about stopped shaking now.' She tried to smile.

'What did they find?' Craig asked, voicing all their curiosities.

'Paperwork, signatures, the contract you signed with the pseudo Eileen Wright. I think they found something that will tell them who the woman was that you met up with.' Lynn fell silent for a moment as a waitress walked over and unloaded a tray of drinks along with a plate of cookies. 'I can't see any way they'll continue chasing you, Craig. He had deposit slips for the business account, and a copy of funds withdrawn from another account that match the five- thousand dollar bribe. I think what happened is he put that five-thousand into the account on the same day he knew the check would be drawn against the account.'

'That might work. When was the check written out? I never did get to see the date on it.'

'The tenth,' Mark answered.

'Of this month? I haven't got the Statement for the month yet, and until that arrived I wouldn't have noticed it. I just do the daily end of business check on the total in the account. It's a thirty second phone call into the bank's computerized system.' Craig explained. 'Well that's not a mistake I'll make again. I could have done a full check, the ten most recent transactions, if I hadn't been taking shortcuts.'

'We learn by our mistakes,' Anita commented tritely.

'I almost didn't get the chance to. Though I have to wonder how he was going to stop the Statement from turning up. Once that arrived I would have had a fighting chance with the case.'

'I'm not sure if he had something planned to cover that, or if he hadn't thought that far,' Lynn admitted. 'We might never know, or it could well turn out the Sheriff has found out. That's something we could end up waiting until the court case to discover.'

'If it gets that far.' Sheriff Johnson suddenly slid into the booth next to Anita. 'Well, I'm sure you'll be pleased to know I'm recommending the case against Craig be dismissed, so Craig, you and McCollum will both need to be at the courthouse tomorrow morning as well. Anita, you'll need to be there to collect your bail money.'

'So what's happening?' she asked, shivering slightly as Craig reached under the table and squeezed her thigh before tracing a light caress along her leg. 'Has he confessed?'

'No, but with what we found in the house, and the few things he's admitted to doing, there's no way Craig remains implicated. You're cleared as far as I'm concerned and will be as far as the paperwork goes tomorrow morning.' He reached for one of the cookies on the plate. 'These are good.' He grinned as he took a second bite.

'So that's it, it's over?' Anita pressed.

'After the court hearing tomorrow, yes, I think it will be. Look, it's been a long day for everyone involved. My suggestion is this – go home, or to Mark's house in your case Lynn. Get some sleep, enjoy a little time together, and then come back in tomorrow morning, get the last of the paperwork out of the way, and you'll be able to put all of this behind you.'

* * *

'I'm not sure if I let you know just how grateful I am that you came to court this morning.' Craig closed the door behind them after they walked into the house. 'It meant a lot to me. I wasn't sure you'd do that.'

'I couldn't leave you to face that on your own.' She slipped her shoes off as she spoke. 'And right now that hot tub is calling to me. Interested?'

'Yes!' He smiled. 'I'll go pull the cover off and turn it on while you go and check through your emails.'

She smiled as he walked out onto the deck and headed straight to her main computer, booting it up before she went to collect several towels. By the time she had those set to one side on the couch her e-mails had downloaded. It didn't take long to go through them, and out of the few e-mails she had only one needed replying to. There was a short message from Sue stating the book release date had not only been confirmed but sent to the stores and the press, allowing for the pre-orders that were so important. As she typed up her reply, she couldn't help but wonder how Sue would react to finding out she was planning on getting married. There was only one way to find out and that would have to wait until they arrived in New York.At least the weight of the court case would be well and truly lifted by that point.

With the towels in hand she walked out onto the deck and stood for a moment watching Craig. He was crouched by the side of the hot tub, checking the temperature, his shirt already stripped off, the same shirt he had been wearing the day before. He hadn't had chance to change with everything that had happened, but they had stopped at his place on the way home so he could grab an overnight bag. He would need to look smart for the hearing the following day, if nothing else than to throw off the impression he didn't care what was happening. That had been the final piece of advice Johnson had offered them as they left the diner.

The wooden deck was still warm from the day, and the sun had yet to leave the sky although long shadows were starting to stretch across the deck. Between the heat from the sun and the relaxing water of the hot tub, this would be the perfect way to end the day.

'Well, how's it going?' she asked, letting her gaze move over his back. 'And I meant to ask, how did you get that scar?'

'It should be ready in a few.' He stood up slowly, shaking off the water from his hand. 'That scar? My first big construction job. The site boss was cutting corners to save money. Some companies will do that and the lucky ones manage to avoid working for those type of people. The scaffolding I was on came loose. He hadn't checked the set up. Instead of making sure he had someone who knew what they were doing setting it up he had a new guy, barely nineteen, do the building. Two of us were standing on it when it collapsed, myself and Ned, the guy who put it up. I walked away, Ned didn't.'

'He died?' she probed, watching his face closely.

'No, he broke his back, permanently damaging his spine. I still keep in contact with him. Ned will be in a wheelchair for the rest of his life.' He walked over and took the towels from her, setting them down in easy reach of the tub. 'He blamed himself for the accident for a long time, but I got him to see it wasn't his fault. The accident put the company into the ground financially, but not until they had been forced to pay out compensation to Ned.'

'What about you?' She traced the outline of the scar.

'I handed mine to Ned. He needed it more than I did. He's a good man, I still keep in contact with him, and I walked away from the accident with a reminder to be careful about who I work for and how to manage a site.'

'That has to be a very hard way to learn a lesson.'

'No more than this business with Ray has been. I've learned to be a lot more careful with the financial aspects of business.'

'I can understand that. I think the tub is ready.' She nodded towards the small curls of steam escaping from the water.

'Then why are we letting it go to waste?' He smiled as he stripped her shirt from her. 'Or were you waiting for a written invitation?' They both laughed as he yanked her jeans down from her hips and tossed them to the floor along with her panties. 'Now this is why I am very glad you live out away from the town, at least this way we aren't about to be disturbed.' He shrugged off his own jeans, tugging off his socks and underpants before stepping into the bubbling warmth of the hot tub with her.

'Have you turned shy all of a sudden?' She stretched, reaching her hands towards the sky as she spoke. 'You didn't seem to mind the idea of other people walking in on us at the park.''That was different.'

'Yes I suppose it was, and in a way exciting, but then so was the Sheriff telling me he had found my panties.'

'He did? Well, at least he didn't know who they belonged to.'

'Yes he did.' She leaned into his arm, feeling him tense at her words. 'Though I was lucky, as he was pretty nice about it. I'm sure mine were not the first pair of panties he found in the park, or elsewhere for that matter.'

'That would be a perk of the job, but for now the only thing I'm interested in is you, me and this hot tub. No, that's not being quite honest. The focus of my attention, my wife to be, is you.' He pinched one of her nipples, rolling it between his thumb and forefinger. 'I want to hear you whimper, moan and plead as I sink my cock into your pussy.' He let go of her nipple, leaving it throbbing. 'Should I tease you before fucking you hard, the way I believe you want me to?'

'No, make love to me,' she begged. 'No more teasing…'

'I will make love to you, now until the end of our days,' he promised, and pulled her onto his lap, nestling her against his hard cock.

Her cunt clenched as she writhed against him, her breasts pressing against his chest. It would have been so easy to rise up a little and lower herself down onto his cock, impaling herself on his throbbing length.

'I love you, Anita, and I will love you until the end of our life together,' he whispered against her lips, teasing them with the tip of his tongue.

She moaned softly, parting her lips, suckling on his

tongue eagerly. She wanted to feel him deep inside her, wanted to feel his erection stretching her open, pushing inside her, thrusting into her. She pushed upwards, raising her ass from his lap, teasing the lips of her sex with the tip of his cock. He groaned against her mouth as she pushed herself down around him, stabbing herself with his hard-on. There would be time for slow later, now she just wanted him, fast and hard. Her hips rocked, her muscles tightening as she felt his thumb touch her clit, teasing it. She circled her hips, her nails clawing into his shoulders.

'Ride me… oh, yes, ride me, baby.' He pushed up to meet her as the water bubbled against them. 'Wicked, wanton, delightful woman, and all mine. God, I love you Anita. I love you!'

She couldn't hold back, she didn't want to hold back, not with her body setting the pace. Her pussy clenched, her clit throbbing with each brush from his thumb. She pressed down against him, her nails digging even deeper into his skin. She wanted him, she needed him, she loved him, she never wanted to be without him again. 'There's something I want to do with you,' she gasped, and pulling herself off his cock she heaved herself out of the water onto the deck. She glanced back at him over her shoulder as she settled onto her hands and knees. 'Fuck me, please.'

'Like this, Anita?' he asked quietly. He climbed out of the tub with her, settling behind her.

'Yes, please, Craig.'

'You're afraid, aren't you?' He slid his hand over the curve of her tight ass cheeks. 'I can feel the fear in you, I can see it in the way you're trembling.'

'Yes,' she admitted, 'I'm afraid, but I want it. I want you.'

'We don't have to do it, not this way. I'm not saying I don't want to do it this way, you look more than tempting, but...' He urged her slowly back into the hot tub, and slid down into the water next to her.

'But?' she whispered.

'I want you, not your fear. Whatever it is about doing it that way that frightens you is something I want to understand first.' He pressed a soft kiss against her lips. 'That's part of being in love, Anita, and I do love you, more than anything else in this world.'

Epilogue

'Are you ready to do this?' she asked, leaning in against him as the elevator continued its journey to the top of the building. 'There's still time to back out. I wouldn't blame you if you did change your mind.'

'Now why would I do that, Anita? I said I'd come with you, and I have no intention of backing out now. I know just how important this is to you.'

He looked so different all dressed up. Even though she had seen him smartly dressed that once in *The Red Deer* she was still used to seeing him mainly in jeans and a t-shirt.

'I'm not sure, but I just wanted to let you know I would

be okay with it if you did decide to pull out.' She smoothed her hands nervously over her dress. It had been a hectic few weeks since Craig was cleared of all charges. One of the hardest things for Lynn to deal with had been finding out her father had raised the money for the scheme by faking her own signature. He'd gone as far as falsifying papers in order to mortgage the house, which had also meant that Craig had had to give all the money back to Lynn since it belonged to her and not her father. What had followed next had surprised them all. Instead of using the money to repay the mortgage, Lynn had used some of it to buy the land around the lake. By the time they returned to Lake Crane, the land Craig had come so close to destroying would be registered as a private nature preserve with access trails to the water. Anita had tried talking Lynn out of it, but once her friend set her mind on something it would have been easier to change the path of a tornado that it would have been to change her mind.

He pulling her closer as the elevator came to a halt. 'Here we go.'

The double doors slid open, letting them out into the hall. 'We just have to step through that door and you'll be entering my life completely, Craig, this is your last chance to back out.'

'Not a chance in hell.' He walked towards the door with his arm still wrapped about her waist. 'Besides, just how scary could they all be?'

Small groups of men and women, mainly women,

where scattered about the large room, posters and books decorating the walls along with photographs of Anita.

'Now those are...' Craig began.

'Just studio shots. They use one of a selection of about ten pictures for the back page of the book. I wish they wouldn't, though, I could do without seeing my own face staring back at me from the back of a book.' She laughed, looking away from the photographs and cover art. 'I hate cameras, I always have.'

'I've no idea why,' he said as he cupped her chin, looking into her eyes. 'You're a beautiful woman, Anita. I've always thought that.'

'Anita!' A voice called out from across the room as other people began moving towards them, smiling.

'Sue.' She moved away from Craig long enough to hug the older woman. 'I'm sorry I'm late, the cab took longer than I thought it would. It's been a while since I was in New York.''And I can see you have another excuse for being this late.' Sue grinned and nodded towards Craig. 'Are you going to introduce me to your escort for tonight, or are you planning on keeping him all to yourself? He certainly looks delicious.'

'Oh, he's not just for tonight, Sue, I'm planning on keeping him to myself for the rest of my life.'

The conversations in the room had died out, and though normally she didn't like being the center of attention, this once Anita was determined to make the most of it.

'What have you been up to?' Sue demanded, her gaze

moving from Craig to Anita and back again. 'I know that look, Anita Burns.'

'Shouldn't I be thanking everyone for attending the launch?' She was enjoying the moment, keeping everyone in suspense. 'Or should we wait until other people arrive?'

'You're a wicked woman!' Sue laughed, shaking her head.

'So I've heard.' She nodded towards Craig, who was enjoying the situation just as much as she was, or so it seemed from his smile. Making the announcement was one of the hardest things she had ever faced in her life, though she had no idea why.

'Oh, go on then, we were going to make the announcements in about twenty minutes, but I don't see any harm in doing them a little earlier.' Sue shook her head good naturedly and walked over to the slightly raised podium, tapping the microphone before she spoke. 'Ladies and gentlemen, if I could have your attention please. Thank you. Before I hand matters over to Anita, I'd like to personally thank you all for agreeing to attend our launch. I've had the pleasure of working with Anita Burns for the past eight years, when she first sent me a manuscript as an uncertain new writer, and I am very pleased to be here as we see the launch of her tenth book, *Love's Sweet Turmoil*. Ladies and Gents, Anita Burns.'

Her stomach churned into tight knots as she stepped up to the microphone. 'Well, it's been a fast couple of years, and those years have seen some interesting changes, but today I'd like to add a new one. Not only am

I very pleased to be here at the launch of this book, but as most of you might have noticed, I'm not here alone.' She glanced towards Craig, beckoning for him to come a little closer. 'I'd like you all to meet Craig Dawson, a gentleman I grew up with, went to school with, one of my best friends, and the man I now call my husband.'

Sue's eyes narrowed, though the smile on her face brightened. 'Are you telling me you'll now be writing as Anita Dawson?'

'I think it would be best if Craig answered that one.' Anita smiled as he walked closer to the microphone. All the tension she had felt when she'd stepped up to speak vanished with his touch.

'Anita and I have already talked about that,' he addressed the room. 'I fell in love with Anita Burns and marriage isn't going to change that. Yes, marrying me changed her name to Dawson, but she'll always be Anita Burns, not just to her readers but to me as well. She's a wonderful woman and I am very proud to finally be able to call her my wife.'

It didn't matter that everyone in the room was watching them, she didn't care as she reached up and wrapped her arms around his neck, pulling his lips down to meet hers. Nothing else mattered beyond the feel of his mouth against hers, the feel of his body pressed close, not even the applause…